MW00932024

2017
To Cayla —

May you have many enjoyable
hours reading about the animals!
I wrote this book for children just like you!

Sally Scott Gwynn

CHRISTMAS 2017
DEAR CAYLA,

HOPE YOU WILL ENJOY THIS BOOK
AND READ IT MANY TIMES THROUGHOUT
YOUR CHILDHOOD AND MAYBE SOMEDAY
TO YOUR CHILDREN.

MERRY CHRISTMAS
& HAPPY NEW YEAR!

LOVE,
GRANDPA & JOYCE

The
TORTOISE
Tales

WRITTEN AND ILLUSTRATED BY
SALLY SCOTT GUYNN

Archway Publishing books may be ordered
through booksellers or by contacting:

Archway Publishing
1663 Liberty Drive
Bloomington, IN 47403
www.archwaypublishing.com
1 (888) 242-5904

Because of the dynamic nature of the Internet, any web addresses or
links contained in this book may have changed since publication and
may no longer be valid. The views expressed in this work are solely those
of the author and do not necessarily reflect the views of the publisher,
and the publisher hereby disclaims any responsibility for them.

Any people depicted in stock imagery provided by Thinkstock are
models, and such images are being used for illustrative purposes only.
Certain stock imagery © Thinkstock.

ISBN: 978-1-4808-5074-3 (sc)
ISBN: 978-1-4808-5072-9 (hc)
ISBN: 978-1-4808-5073-6 (e)

Library of Congress Control Number: 2017955093

Print information available on the last page.

Archway Publishing rev. date: 10/27/2017

For Mae Wallace, Walker, Bo and Sebastian

ACKNOWLEDGMENTS

While writing this book many people blessed me with their encouragement. My heart is full of gratitude for their support. I wish to thank in particular my husband, Dwight Guynn, my four constantly inspirational grandchildren, Mae Wallace, Walker, Bo, and Sebastian, and my dear friend, Judy Stokes. I'll also remain forever grateful for the brilliant feedback I received from my colleagues in the *Aspiring Writers' Critique Class* at the Lifelong Learning Institute in Midlothian, Virginia, namely Pat Parsons, Marya Dull, Hal Cauthen, Bob Ferguson and, most especially, the indomitable Dorothy Moses. Their keen yet kind critique made all the difference.

CONTENTS

Introduction xi

Tale 1: Ezra 1

Tale 2: The Funky Monkey 17

Tale 3: The Boy and the Dragon 33

Tale 4: Charles Bronson and the Crows 49

Tale 5: The Three Little Caddisflies 65

Tale 6: Stinky–The Goat Who Would Be Cow 87

Tale 7: The Chameleon's New Smile 105

Tale 8: White Feathers 117

Tale 9: The Blue Light Mystery 131

Noodle Joggers..155

More About the Author............................171

INTRODUCTION

Nine stories await, herein, ready to challenge your imagination should you dare to open your mind and virtually take a ride on the back of a giant old tortoise who really knows some stuff.

My tortoise friend swore his unusual animal tales were mostly true—at least parts of them. You'll have to make up your own mind about that. Each story offers both young readers and adults alike insights for life and an inside view of the wonders of nature.

The stories follow in no particular order with one exception—*Tale One: Ezra.* By reading the first tale first, you meet the storyteller up close and personal and ready yourself for the remaining stories. *Juicy Animal Facts* follow each story and offer expanded explanations to special terms. At the end of the book an additional section titled *Noodle Joggers* presents ideas from each of the stories to challenge your brain and solicit discussion.

In the pages ahead, you'll meet animal characters you're not likely to forget. Their life changing situations, not too unlike our own in many respects, come packed full of drama and suspense, wisdom and courage, and plenty to make you smile.

— *Sally Scott Guynn*

EZRA

The old tortoise made his way carefully and slowly up the steep, twisting, narrow path he knew so well. The path led from woods to the top of the knoll where he could look out and see far and wide. He moved slowly because he was, after all, a tortoise. And he moved slowly because he was really old—at least 130 years old at last count.

The width of the well-worn path offered barely enough space for the tortoise to fit, and it had no paved asphalt overtop either. No sir. Littered with sticks, acorns, rocks, and hardened blobs of dirt from rains past, the path held its own history.

The tortoise had his work cut out for him. As he climbed, he mumbled silently now to himself revealing a glimpse of his usual wit and sense of humor, *"Just another challenge, pay it no mind; stay on purpose and be glad I'm at least not blind."* And on the ancient reptile trudged.

Not too far away a young girl named Sally Scott also

roamed, as was her custom. She adored the hills and the wonderful woods. Already she'd discovered a bird's nest with three small sky blue eggs in it, a nice smooth, flat black rock in the creek, and animal tracks in the mud of some unknown furry type of critter, most likely a raccoon best she could figure. She carefully left the treasures as she'd found them and continued on her way.

When afternoon came Sally Scott decided to visit a certain place she called her lookout point and enjoy the view there like she'd done so many times before. After hiking to the top she sat down on a big rock to rest and take in the magnificent view. She slowly breathed in the clean smells of the pines and fresh air. She hadn't sat for very long when she thought she felt the rock beneath her move.

"*Whaaat?*" she asked herself out loud trying her best to convince herself she'd only imagined movement.

She gingerly scooted off the big rock and stood there staring at it for a moment or two. Puzzled, she scanned it for details, wanting to make sure she wasn't losing her mind or something. But before another minute passed, the strangest scene began unfolding before her. The big rock began to grow four large legs covered all over with big creepy scales and some seriously long claws at the ends!

Sally Scott went mute like a clam. She couldn't get a single word out, or scream, or make any sound of any description. Utter surprise totally captured her, and she remained glued to silently and intently watching the "rock." Then a large, peculiar looking head popped out of the rock and looked back at her.

If that wasn't remarkable enough, the truly spectacular event unfolding in front of her suddenly became even more extraordinary when she heard a voice speak to her –but she heard it *inside* her head instead of with her ears.

The mysterious voice said: *"Don't be afraid my dear. I'm sure you've realized by now this rock is clearly not a rock at all. It must be most discombobulating to you. I apologize for that, I really do. Let me introduce myself. My name is Ezra, although most of the animals just call me "E-Z" for short. What's your name?"*

While still somewhat in shock Sally Scott gradually began to calm down. The animal's voice in her head sounded very gentle and friendly and soothing. She decided to answer him, speaking as loudly and as bravely as she could muster. *"Hello. My name is Sally Scott. You're the biggest, uh, turtle I've ever seen. I didn't know turtles could get this big! How are you able to speak to me like this? It's weird."*

"First, I'm a tortoise, not a turtle. I've never been able to 'mind transfer' my thoughts to a human before," the old tortoise replied, speaking very slowly and clearly. *"You're the first. You must be very comfortable in the woods and around wild things in wild places. And you must have a kind spirit too. Is that right?"* he asked, again without uttering any sound whatsoever through his mouth but looking at her intently all the while.

"Yes, I suppose you could describe me that way," Sally Scott answered, privately thinking all the while how relieved she was no one was around to hear her talking to a giant tortoise.

Ezra continued, *"Many years ago back east in Virginia, a Native American Medicine Man gave me the gift of 'mind transfer' and made me promise to pass on my stories about animals, but only to a human with the right heart spirit. Such a person would be able to hear my most peculiar way of communicating."* Then he added, *"And he chose **me** to be the storyteller instead of the know-it-all owl. I was better at keeping a secret."*

Eventually, the tortoise's voice inside her head sounded pretty normal to her. And she noticed more excitement in his "voice," too. Ezra continued: *"I'm so happy to finally be able to 'talk' with a human and not just waste time trying to converse with dumb rabbits or way too busy raccoons and such. As I said, I'm what's known as 'a storyteller' and I've been saving up my animal stories for a very long time with no one to tell them to until now."*

Sally Scott could hardly believe what she was *hearing.* She remained amazed but not scared at all and wasted not a minute more in responding back to him since one of her most favorite things was learning about animals.

*"I would absolutely **love** to hear your stories. I'd be most honored in fact. But could you first tell me a little more about yourself? It's not every day I meet a giant tortoise, much less a talking one!"* she said.

And that's how their most odd friendship began.

They'd regularly meet in the same patch of woods and continue their most grand conversations. And Sally Scott learned a lot more from Ezra about turtles versus tortoises. Ezra, clearly, was a tortoise–a very large, very old tortoise. Unlike turtles, Ezra couldn't swim a lick. And like all tortoises, he was born on land and had remained a landlubber for all his 130+ years.

One of the earliest, most impressive things Sally Scott observed about her unusual new friend was the great contrast between his calm, non-aggressive manner compared with how big and how strong he was. Ezra moved slowly and deliberately on thick, muscular legs that looked more like tree trunks at first glance. His claws made excellent digging tools, his jaws worked like a steel trap, and he didn't tire easily. His laser sharp memory equaled his dry clever wit, too. He also managed carrying a giant-sized, hard shell across his back. It looked like a patchwork quilt of large thickened scales.

When her curiosity got the best of her she asked him about it one day. *"Can you tell me about the shell on your back? Is it heavy? Can you crawl out of it? Have you always had it?"* she asked.

If Ezra could've managed a smile he most certainly would have hearing the girl's questions, but his stiff reptile scales prevented any facial expressions like smiling. He blinked a couple of times and then happily answered Sally Scott's questions one by one.

"The shell on my back is actually my skeleton. It's a

THE OLD TORTOISE REALLY KNOWS SOME STUFF

part of me, more like a patchwork quilt of bones fused together than scales or a true shell. I think of it as wearing good armor. My muscles attach to it like your muscles attach to your bones so you can move. A clam has a shell but it can't move around like I can. My type of 'shell' is what all tortoises have. It protects me from weather and wannabe enemies too, but I'm not able to crawl out of it. It's like having my body and my home in one. It's really strong and heavy," he answered, then quickly added, "Wanna take a ride on it?"

The two of them made quite a pair, the girl riding atop Ezra's back listening to his animal stories and the extraordinary old tortoise so glad he'd finally found a special friend to "talk" to. Sally Scott asked him many more questions and he always patiently answered them. On one occasion as they walked along conversing with her on his back, she asked him, "Where do you live, Ezra?"

"The better question for me might be, 'Where **haven't** I lived?'" he answered.

"Okay, **E-Z**, where did you **first** live?" she clarified.

"I spent my early years in a place they still call Virginia, but I didn't begin my life there," he said.

"Would you tell me about where you first lived? And I'm also curious about why you left?" she asked.

The rest of the afternoon Ezra described his early life and some of his journey. "I first lived with many other big tortoises on a lovely island far, far away. I remember how nice and warm it felt there all the time. But one day a *great many of us were captured by humans who carried big knives between their teeth, wore bandanas on their heads and yelled an awful lot. They put us in the belly of their big ship and held us prisoner there with nothing to drink or eat as we sailed on a vast ocean for a very long time.*

"What?" Sally Scott blurted out. "I can't imagine such a nightmare! How did you endure it?"

"Because we were tortoises we made no noise. We didn't annoy anybody," Ezra explained. "But every now and then one or two of the humans came down the ladder to our dark cellar and killed one of the tortoises! Later we could smell them cooking it to feed their crew!"

"Oh my goodness, Ezra, that's just so horrible! How'd you ever get freed from that?" Sally Scott cried out.

Ezra took his time explaining. "After a while the big ship grew heavy from all the stuff the humans had been taking on from one place and another. One day as the ship sailed within sight of a broad beach of land, it began to scrape bottom in the shallows. So to lighten their ship the humans began throwing cargo overboard. Then they threw many of us tortoises overboard too and sailed away while we tried in vain to keep from sinking.

I was lucky. Somehow I managed to grab and hang onto some wooden planks and small barrels tied together. I floated alongside, holding on to the makeshift raft until the tides took me right up onto a wide beach of Virginia where I lived for many more years."

Sally Scott could tell how Ezra must have loved living in Virginia. He described to her how he'd seen vast open country and great virgin forests there. No railroads or telephone poles or big wide roadways spoiled the view. White humans were just beginning to build their many towns and such.

"You know, back then the entire eastern part of the big land you call America had vast forests of giant chestnut trees. The chestnut trees were the kings of the forests in the east. They literally carpeted the land. Many believed a squirrel could travel from Maine to Alabama back then without ever having to leave the treetops of those mighty chestnut trees and never having to touch the ground."

Simply enthralled hearing Ezra describe the way it used to be, Sally Scott tried hard to keep from interrupting him with her questions. *"I'll bet those trees gave plenty of nuts for you and many other animals and many places to live, too. Right?"*

"Yes. The chestnut trees were truly magnificent in so many ways. And some other wild types of giants also lived in Virginia back in those early days. I saw plenty of buffalo, elk, wolves, and cougars. They roamed all over in the east back then in great numbers. And passenger pigeons were as plentiful as seagulls at beaches today! I decided to leave the east coast when so many numbers of the great wild animals began to dwindle as more and more humans arrived."

"Wow! I never knew this! Today, animals like elk and wolves are mostly found in the western parts of the U.S. I've heard some have been brought back from the west to parts of the east," Sally Scott said, hardly able to contain herself. *"And I'd definitely never before heard about*

those great chestnut trees. I don't ever remember seeing one either."

"That's right, girl. The giant chestnut trees began to die one by one from a mysterious blight that came from chestnut trees brought here from China. That's when I began my slow journey west, munching on chestnuts off the ground until there simply were no more."

Sally Scott begged Ezra to tell her one story after another about animals from his many exploits. She promised him she'd faithfully write them all down just as he told them, and one day she'd make them part of a book for children. Ezra shared each of his memories with the same great excitement as the girl had hearing them.

For openers, Ezra shared two little, relatively unknown stories. The first story featured an enormous fish and the second one told of whales teaching something to other animals. Ezra swore they were mostly true as he set himself down to begin his first story:

"Okay, Sally Scott. My first very short story for you describes a big event in Virginia when I lived there long ago. A wonderful river there, the James River, flowed from the mountains to the ocean. Every year near Richmond a certain Native American tribe, the Pamunkey, held a rite of passage in that river for their young men to prove their bravery and broadcast their manhood. The young men would ride upon the backs of giant sturgeon fish that lived in the Atlantic Ocean but returned each year in great numbers to the freshwaters of their birthplace in the James and York Rivers.

Riding Giant Sturgeon Back in the Old Days

More than twice the size of a human, these fish had barely changed since prehistoric times. They looked a lot like a stegosaurus dinosaur but with fins and armored with five rows of bony plates like a dragon might look. Normally rather gentle in nature, once a human began to ride them the giants went crazy, jumping way out of the water and thrashing about like wild sea monsters or a bucking bull at a rodeo trying to unseat his rider. T'was most exciting to witness I can assure you," Ezra said as he ended the little story.

"For real?" Sally asked in disbelief, her mouth gaping open.

"Yeah, for real. It's been recorded in history. The sturgeon stopped coming up into Virginia's rivers for many years but have been making a promising comeback in this 21st century," Ezra answered matter-of-factly.

Almost before Sally Scott had time to reset her brain to take in any more incredible scenes from the old tortoise's memories, he'd geared up and began another.

"My next little story for you is about whales off the east coast of the great America. They taught the giant elk, large deer-like beasts living in the east back then how to sing to each other. Whales actually sing to each other underwater in the oceans, you know. To this day in America's west, every fall when the aspens and the cottonwood trees turn all yellow in the Rocky Mountains, you can hear the bull elk singing the whale's songs. Their sad-sounding songs ring out across the mountains to help the elk choose their mates and create their own herds."

"*That one for real too?*" Sally asked again.

"*Well, I'll leave that up to you to sort out, but personally I think it makes a lot of sense,*" Ezra replied.

While riding on his back Sally Scott captured eight more of Ezra's animal stories and wrote them down as separate tales in the pages following just for you.

Juicy Animal Facts From
Tale One: *Ezra*

Turtles & Tortoises—are like cousins. Turtles and tortoises both are reptiles, as are snakes and lizards. Turtles live on land and breathe air but they also can stay submerged underwater holding their breath for long periods of time. Because turtles live in both water and land, they are said to be amphibious. Tortoises only live on land, and the giant tortoises are the largest, cold-blooded animals on the planet.

Skeleton—is the body's bony support system of many groups of animals including fish, reptiles, birds and mammals.

Chestnut tree—was the dominant large tree in the southeastern part of the U.S. prior to mid-20th century that provided great habitat for wildlife and contributed greatly to the U.S. economy from the sale and use of its wood.

Buffalo, elk, wolves & cougars—are animals that lived in great numbers throughout America before it was fully colonized, but today they are found mostly in the western U.S.

Passenger pigeons—were plentiful game birds throughout the U.S. in the early 1800s and early 20th century. Passenger pigeons, possibly the most abundant bird on the planet at one time, now are extinct from un-regulated hunting and over-harvesting of mature forests, their primary habitat. Today, the white-crowned pigeons of the Caribbean also face similar extinction. The demise of the passenger pigeon offers us a profound lesson in conservation biology: *"It's not always necessary to kill the last pair of a species to force its extinction."* In other words, cutting down old forests may cause the animals that depend on old trees to also die off.

Chestnut blight—is a particular fungus infection from China that infected the highly valued American Chestnut tree beginning in the early 1900s and resulted in a complete wipeout of the trees (3-4 billion trees within

50 years!). Young shoots still arise today from old roots but live only until they become young trees and then they too die from the disease. Research continues to try to find a cure.

Prehistoric—refers to a time occurring before humans recorded and wrote things down.

THE FUNKY MONKEY

As Ezra began telling his first major story to the girl on his back, she remained surprised at how distinct and normal his voice sounded inside her head yet no outside sound of him could be heard through her ears. And it all happened amazingly with no effort on her part whatsoever. By the excitement in the old tortoise's words she knew he was most happy to share another story with her. Clearly, his memories gave him a second pair of eyes to be able to describe in such great detail what he could see in his recollection.

The giant cat was back. Slowly, silently, almost gliding through the dark thick jungle he moved with purpose and precision, blending in almost completely with the night forest. Then, almost at once as if on command, all the noises of all the jungle creatures stopped.

Even the air stood still. It felt like just before a summer storm sometimes. It seemed as if all were holding their breath waiting for *him* to pass. And the silence began to scream danger.

But he was on a hunt and nothing would get in his way or cause him to just pass on by. With each careful, deliberate step his large furry paws whispered a soft thud on the huge palm leaves carpeting the jungle floor. All the sound even the sharpest of ears could hear that moonless night.

He was Somat (*pronounced So māht)*–Somat the jaguar. And he was most definitely back!

The blackest fur you ever saw on a cat covered his sleek muscular body—glistening, inky black fur obscuring the mosaic of leopard spots on his skin beneath, and blurring the boundaries between the night's darkness and the cat's imposing body.

Only one exception escaped the darkness–two very yellow, penetrating eyes–glowing portals they were … *his* portals for reaching deep into the night.

And every now and then he'd silently open his mouth wide as it could go, quickly dissolving the night's inky darkness to reveal his set of large, very white, very sharp pointy teeth. Perhaps it was this impressive weaponry of his that made it feel just so good to try and show them off in spite of the pitch black darkness surrounding him.

Somat stopped, sniffing the air again for any telltale scent of his intended prey. He arched his back, tilted his head slightly and sniffed a good, long, unhurried sniff with the most powerful sensory organ he possessed–his nose. While he waited and sniffed, his long, thick, graceful black tail twitched back and forth nervously.

For a moment or two he pondered again how much he truly hated the waiting part. Then suddenly there it was–a most distinct smell floating in the air–the invisible, telltale scent-cloud of monkeys!

Instinct kicked in and Somat instantly went into crawl position. Crouched almost flat to the ground he slithered along like a reptile, his body fully tensed up. He could wait no longer.

An entire monkey troop lay sleeping, draped over branches high up in the tallest of several towering trees. *"Zzzzzzzzz. Zzzzzzzzz.* Burp! *Zzzz.* Scratch! *Zzzzz."*

All slept and snored except for one that is–one very irritated, cross little monkey who'd been trying to sleep next to another monkey named Melton, but Melton's snoring kept waking him up. Besides his snoring, Melton was widely known, among other things, for his unpleasant body odor. Getting an up-close whiff of him every time whenever one of the monkeys awakened during the night made it much more difficult for them to get back to sleep again.

"C'mon, Smelly," whined the sleepy monkey. *"Roll over or do* **something**–**ANYTHING**. *I've got to get some sleep!"*

Meanwhile, Somat had begun his silent ascent easily digging his big claws into the rough bark of a tree closest

SOMAT STALKS MONKEY TROOP

to the monkeys. A skillful predator, he took care to stay in stealth mode while he climbed upward. But every now and then as he thought about the delicious morsels awaiting him, he simply couldn't hold back sliding his tongue across his upper lip and swallowing hard.

When Somat reached a branch close to the treetop he found it easily within jumping distance to the group of sleeping monkeys. Then two things happened almost simultaneously. The cat's intended target, Melton, rolled over at the exact moment the huge cat leaped through the air from his tree limb, screaming a ferocious, blood curdling roar out into the jungle night!

"Roooooooooaaaarrrrrrrrr !"

But, alas, Somat realized too late that his target monkey had suddenly changed his sleeping position. To make matters worse, in the middle of his dramatic leap through the air, Somat tried to correct his direction, but guessed incorrectly and fell helplessly out of the tree and into a thorn bush on the ground below. Long, needle-like thorns pierced him turning his lips and nose into a painful pincushion.

"Roooaaaaarrrrrrffff!" he bellowed in pain, his sensitive nose immediately beginning to swell like a balloon filling with air. Somat batted furiously at the thorns with his paws, then began rubbing his face against the broad, cool, smooth leaves of nearby plants. He slunk off into the night while his nose continued to swell.

Now fully awakened, all the monkeys realized with

SOMAT GETS A THORNY NOSE

horror what had almost happened. Instantly they scattered in different directions and hid, their entire bodies shaking with the monkey shivers in spite of their furry skins. After waiting a safe time, one by one they slowly regrouped.

"Where's that Smelly Melly gone now? Mellllllton, you come here right now! Front and center, mister! We need to talk!" shouted the alpha monkey of the troop.

Now, just to be clear, they called Melton *"Smelly Melly"* for a very good reason. The simple truth: he just hated keeping clean. When all the other monkeys in the troop sat around in the afternoon sun, grooming each other, searching for and picking at the pesky bugs in each other's fur, Melton went off swinging through the trees looking for yummy mangoes, a fruit favorite. And when the troop slipped into the creek to bathe and swim in its watery eddies, Melton was nowhere to be found.

"I don't like the water and I don't like other monkeys always touching me and getting in my face!" Melton would always say under his breath.

So it didn't take long before all the other monkeys began to call him *"Smelly Melly"* instead of Melton. And like most nicknames, it stuck.

"Mellllllton! Smelly Melly! You come here right now!" yelled out the alpha monkey for the second time.

And this time Melton showed himself. *"Yes sir?"* he answered quietly, looking down at his feet and sort of kicking at his tail.

"Melton, this is it. You hear me? We're just not going to

put up with the consequences of your unacceptable personal hygiene any longer. We've given you a million warnings, Smelly. But you just keep blowing us off. The bottom line, Melton, is, well, you smell! You stay dirty and you smell really bad and you put us all in danger. Like tonight for example. How do you think Somat knew where to find us in the pitch dark of night? **YOU**, that's how! Your smell led him right to us. And this is not the first time is it, Melton? No, it most definitely is not. But it's going to be the last time and that's certain!"

"Okay. I'll get cleaned up, whatever," Melton offered half-heartedly. "You don't need to get so riled up about it."

"Not this time, Melton," said the alpha. "You'd just end up again going right back to not washing and grooming. Your dirtiness has become a habit with you, Melton. You've become a funky monkey! And that, as you well know, is not only unpleasant to the rest of us, it also makes us all vulnerable–easy prey we become. Somat can find us anytime he needs a snack—just follow the Smelly Melly, funky monkey trail! No problem-o! No, Melton, you'll have to leave us. I'm sorry. There's no other way."

The alpha had spoken. His word in the troop was final. There would be no point in trying to argue with him. Melton's head lowered and then drooped down even more as he slowly walked down the path and out into the waiting jungle.

"What am I going to do?" he thought. "How will I make it all alone out here?" Melton didn't know what he felt more—scared or worried. But he knew for sure he felt both of those feelings. He walked along missing the others in his troop more than he'd ever thought possible.

Meanwhile, Somat's nose had swollen up quite badly from the thorns and now caused him great difficulty breathing. He had to breathe through his mouth only, and with his nose so swollen it caused a weird sound every time he sucked air in and out.

"Ssssshhhhsssshhhhh. Ssssssshhhhsssshhhhh," he noisily breathed as he moved through the jungle. The good news for the monkeys was now the troop could hear him coming. Try as he might over the next few weeks, Somat could not surprise attack any of the monkeys.

With Melton gone and the jaguar's noisy breathing acting like an alarm system, the monkey troop enjoyed their newfound safety. They danced, blew mango seeds at each other, chased butterflies, and scratched in the sun. Life was good. But as time passed, the monkeys grew over confident. They forgot the cardinal monkey rule—"Always be on guard!"

Some distance away and quite alone, Melton spent every moment of daylight searching for food. Finding food had become much harder to do without the others. "If only the troop were here to help me get those banana bunches over there", or "I could get those mangoes a lot easier if I had the others here," Melton whined out loud to himself as he groped along.

One day Melton spied a bush growing by the river's edge. Its limbs drooped slightly, loaded down from the weight of its fruit. Like finding unlimited candy, Melton smacked his lips and ran to the bush grabbing as big a handful of the delicious fruits as he could. He stuffed them in his mouth and quickly grabbed another handful and then another. Then, just as he stretched out reaching for one final grab, he suddenly lost his balance and tumbled down the steep riverbank and into the swiftly moving waters below.

"Help! Help!" he screamed. *"Quick, save me somebody!"* But the mighty roar of the river swallowed up the sound of his voice and made futile any attempts to call for help.

Somehow Melton managed to stay afloat remarkably well until he hit a waterfall. Before he knew what was happening, over he went. Head over toe, round and round, the water tossed him about like a little monkey dishrag.

And then in the midst of all this a very peculiar thing began to happen to him, most peculiar indeed. He realized he actually felt lighter. As the sheer force of the flowing water swept the dirt and matted leaves and stickers from his body, he felt freed. And, surprisingly, the water felt good too.

He kicked his monkey feet and swam as hard as he could to the waters' edge. There he managed to grab hold to a low-hanging tree limb. He pulled and pulled it with all his might. He even used his tail to help grab and pull until he finally crawled out of the river.

"I can't believe I survived that!" he cried out happily.

"*I would love to be able to tell the others about …*" his voice trailing off. Melton stopped still, straining to hear. He thought he could hear monkey sounds and they didn't sound too far away.

"*Could I be back near my troop again?*" he wondered. "*It's louder now. Yes, I do believe it's definitely monkey sounds I'm hearing!*"

He eagerly climbed a tall mango tree and spied his old troop clearly from the hundred foot high perch. The monkeys bathed in a small pool of water, laughing and playing. Oddly, he saw no guard monkey on duty. He looked around a little more and then his eyes fixed on a black object. It was *him*, Somat, watching *them*! Partially hidden by dense jungle vegetation, Somat lay crouched only a few yards away from the unsuspecting monkeys.

"*I've got to do something!*" Melton cried to himself. He thought for a moment or two then added, "*I've got it!*" In the blink of an eye, Melton armed himself with two big mangoes he plucked right from the top of the tree he sat in. He drew his arms way back and hurled the fruit down like a discus, aiming right at the head of the huge cat who waited in deadly readiness.

"*Kabam!*" the mangoes broadcast as they hit dead on their target.

The jaguar shook his head, stood up, and staggered dizzily over to the edge of the riverbank. Smelly watched in amazement as the big cat next simply stepped out onto nothing but air. Somat careened down the slope madly scratching at the air all the while until he plunged into the river with a huge splash. The fast flowing waters offered no mercy, immediately sweeping him downstream and out of sight in just minutes.

Melton ran to see if everyone in the troop was okay. He completely forgot about being a monkey in exile. All the other monkeys in the troop ran to meet him, too, thanking him over and over again for saving them from another close call with Somat.

Finally, the alpha monkey also approached Melton and spoke. *"Melton, what a brave and caring thing you just did for us. We thank you. But Melton, what has happened to you?"* The alpha looked Melton up and down and then questioned him again, *"You no longer smell! What happened to Melvin the funky monkey?"*

"Let's just say I had a life-changing experience down there in the river myself. An experience freeing me from any funkiness!" Melton answered, smiling and his face reddening a little.

"Well, we all welcome you back," the alpha said rather emphatically as he held out his arms wide to Melton.

That's how the story ends. Melton became much loved, much cleaner, and well known far and wide for his bravery. And he was never called Smelly Melly, the funky monkey again.

MOST EVERYONE THOUGHT, "GOODBYE SMELLY
MELLY, HELLO MARVELOUS MELTON!"

Juicy Animal Facts From Tale Two: *The Funky Monkey*

Panthers—make up the third biggest cat group after lions and tigers; "panther" refers to black leopards in eastern countries and black jaguars in the Americas.

Jungle—is a type of tropical, hot ecosystem with dense plants and trees.

Predator—is the term for an animal that hunts/kills other animals for food.

Troop—is a small group or community of monkeys.

Alpha—is the top, oldest or most powerful leader within a group of animals who live together closely such as monkeys, wolves, elephants, etc. The alpha's role is to protect, keep the peace, and determine where to find food.

Mangoes—are an ancient, juicy, tangy-sweet tropical stone fruit that is yellow to red when ripe and grows on trees from 100 to 130 feet tall.

TALE THREE

THE BOY AND THE DRAGON

At this point in the storytelling, Ezra, the ole tortoise leaned his head in a little closer and let the girl know this next story would be a little different. Sally Scott tried closing her eyes so she could concentrate better on the forthcoming story.

Long, long ago, before such modern times as now, there lived a spunky little boy named Beaulion, or just Bo for short. Bo had a great head of dark brown wavy hair and always wore a cool leather cord around his neck with a carving of a dragon on it. It was his most precious possession. His keen mind and lively imagination were surpassed only by his great love of animals.

Bo always wondered about the world. He asked lots of questions and believed anything was possible. He'd ask things like: *"Why do lightning bugs light up?"* and *"How does it know when to rain?"* and on and on. He'd asked what seemed like everything on his mind. Sometimes he got answers but often his parents and the elders in his small village didn't know the answers and politely shushed him away.

Sometimes he laid his head down and put his ear right next to the ground, listening as hard as he could for faraway, mysterious sounds. He'd say, *"You never know what you might hear. Maybe you'll hear a giant walking somewhere far away!"*

You see, Bo had this kind of knowing way down deep. He could just sense stuff. He felt a whole lot more awaited him in his great, big, mysterious world than he knew. More than anyone knew most likely. And it was terribly exciting.

Bo loved to cloud-watch, too. He'd pick out animals in the cloud shapes as they gently floated across the sky and then disappeared just as quickly. One shape in the clouds he tried his very hardest to see—that shape for him the most fun of all the critters to imagine. I bet you can't guess what it was. It was the shape of a dragon.

Bo had heard folks talking about dragons, but it was always dragons in some place far away and long ago like in the ancient days. Bo had never known anyone who'd ever actually seen or heard a real dragon.

"So what?" he'd say to himself. *"It's a known fact some lizards long ago were giants with venom from their mouths*

that burned like fire. And some eels in the oceans even today can shock you in the water. So, why not dragons?"

Bo refused to limit himself. Even when it came to his thinking, he didn't like it one tiny bit. His imagination and game playing didn't end when the sun went down either. Just as Bo found fun things to do during the day, he also enjoyed some harmless but private things at night sometimes.

For example, he'd put his pillow in the windowsill and stick his head out the window and look up at the night sky. You know what he'd be looking for? He looked for stars—certain stars outlining a dragon's body high above in the inky dark sky of night.

"Just like connect-the-dots," he'd smile and say. *"Connect the right star dots and you can see a dragon sure as anything!"*

Sometimes when nobody saw, he'd take a small, metal bucket and add a glowing hot ember from the fireplace at home and he'd take off to his river spot, his "thinking place" he called it. He'd pick up some little twigs scattered around on the ground and put them right on top of the hot ember. Then he'd blow on it until he had a little fire going in his bucket. He'd sit down next to the bucket real close and enjoy the warmth of the fire while he listened to the sounds of the animals in the night.

One of his favorites came from the Whip-poor-will. That bird started up real early in the evening all energetic like and singing rapid-fire, *"Whippoorwill, Whippoorwill, Whippoorwill, Whippoorwill!"* It would sing out so fast you could hardly make out the words. And he'd sing with all his heart. Later at home towards the middle of the night, if Bo happened to wake up, he noticed the same bird sounded less energetic and more like: *"Whiipweel … Whiipweel."*

By early morning, just before the sun rose, that same determined little bird sounded plumb tuckered out. Bo could still hear him all right, poor thing, but by then the bird sounded real, real slow and more like: *"Wheeep---weee. Wheeep---weee."* It always made Bo smile. He'd think to himself, *"That bird might get real tuckered out but he never gives up! I respect that."*

Sometimes on clear evenings Bo listened to the frogs talking to each other. He could make out different kinds of frog talk. *"Rrribit, Rrribit, Rrribit,"* cried out the pond frogs. Or he might hear the high-pitched *"Peep, peep. Peep, peep"* of the tree frogs or the deep resonate *"Whooaap, Whooaap"* of the bullfrogs. Together, their funny voices sounded like some kind of weird, offbeat musical band.

The owl in the big tree down by the river kept calling out all creepy sounding … like he'd missed something, Bo thought. *"Who-Whooooo. Who-Whooooo,"* the owl hooted. Bo respected all the animals and loved listening to them talking to each other night or day.

One night in particular as Bo walked along next to the river, he heard a most unusual noise. It sounded like two huge tree limbs rubbing against each other in the wind, the noise high-pitched and pretty loud. He wondered if the sound came from somewhere far off and merely carried to him by the water of the river. Curious as always, Bo couldn't resist walking on a bit more in the direction of the sound.

Eventually he saw an old stone bridge crossing over the river just ahead. He stopped still as a post and strained his ears for a moment or two trying to locate the direction of the sound's source. He walked towards the bridge and found it a little unsettling how much louder the sound grew once he got closer to the bridge. He suspected the sound might actually be coming from *under* the bridge.

He couldn't resist calling out something so he gently cried out, *"Hello? Is anyone there? Is something the matter? Do you need help?"*

Silence.

"Hello?" he called again softly. *"Please come out so I can see you. I won't hurt you. I promise."*

"No," came a voice back suddenly from under the bridge. *"I can't."*

"Why not?" Bo asked excitedly.

"I'm too embarrassed," the mysterious voice answered.

"What are you embarrassed about?" Bo questioned further.

"I'm embarrassed because my fire's burned out that's why!" the voice answered again, sounding a little irritated.

"But I don't understand," Bo replied. *"Why would your fire being burned out, whatever **that** means, cause you to be embarrassed? I am, after all, just a kid. More information please."*

*"Alright, **OKAY**! If you **MUST** know, I **SIMPLY** cannot let anyone see me like this, all burned out and all, because it's **JUST** not fitting for a dragon to be seen like that,"* the voice blurted out, making the high pitched sound even louder.

"Huh?" croaked Bo, covering his ears with his hands. *"Did you say **DRAGON**? As in D-R-A-G-O-N? As in great-big-huge-winged-lizard-thingie with glowing eyes and a big pointy tail and teeth and creepy scaly skin and really bad fire breath? Like that kind of dragon?"*

"Yeah, that pretty much describes me, I guess," the voice answered back flatly.

"Well you certainly don't need to be embarrassed in front of me that's for sure! I'd be most honored to meet you face to face, Mr. Dragon. It doesn't matter what kind of problem you're having, you see, I really love animals, all kinds of animals, and I've always believed in dragons too," Bo said, his excitement mounting by the minute. *"I'm what you might call a possibility thinker! Oh, please come out, Mr. Dragon!"*

To his surprise, out from the darkness under the bridge came a rustling sound, like leaves and twigs and rocks and such moving around. And then suddenly there he was—all thirty feet of him! His big reddish colored head drooped way down and his eyes shut closed. He moved, more like shuffled, very, very slowly up to where Bo stood with his boy mouth hanging dumbly wide open.

Bo started talking to the giant creature almost

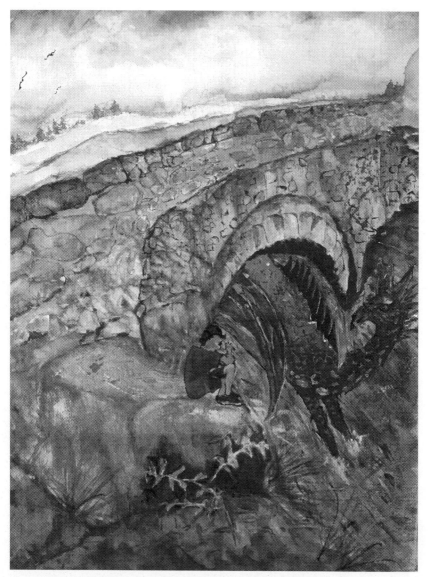

BO AND LONG MEET AT THE BRIDGE

singing-like with his voice oh-so-gentle. *"Its okay. Take your time. When you're ready, just tell me what's wrong. I'm going to help you, Mr. Dragon, but I'm going to need to know a few more details first."*

The dragon began moving himself around and round in a circle trying his best to get his enormous tail into a comfortable position so he could lie down without gouging himself with one of the pointed spikes running down his back and tail.

After much concerted effort he finally managed a suitable position, half his body out and half his huge body remaining under the bridge. Then he slowly raised his head up, opened his great big, dimly glowing eyes, and stared directly at Bo, calmly asking, *"How could **you possibly** help me?"*

"Well, I don't know how yet," Bo said. *"That's why I need you to tell me exactly why you're so upset. What did you mean when you said you were 'burned out?"*

"Precisely it," said the Dragon. *"Precisely."*

*"But what is **it**, precisely?"* struggled Bo.

*"Most precisely **it** is my fire. The combustion I blow out of my mouth like any decent dragon—well, mine has utterly burned out. **I - have - no - fire - left!** I'm **fireless!**"* the dragon moaned.

"Oh, gosh, that does sound serious. May I know your name?" Bo asked politely.

"I am called 'Long," the dragon answered rather formally.

"What a funny name," Bo chuckled. *"I guess with a*

last name like '**dragon**', '**Long**' is a lot better than being called '**short**', huh? Ha, ha, ha."

"The name Long means dragon in Chinese," the huge animal scowled down at Bo. "Dragons share a long and proud history in the faraway land of China."

"Really? Well, I don't live in China but I have two names too!" Bo said proudly. "One is 'Bo' and the other is my family name, 'Angus'. It's Scottish. See? We both have two names. Cool," Bo happily declared. "But now lets try and figure out how we solve your problem."

After some time had passed and Bo had thought hard about the problem, he spoke again to the dragon saying, "I know you need fire, right? Well, I just happen to have in my bucket right here this hot coal from my mother's fire-place. Why don't you blow on it a couple of times to get it all glowing hot and red and then inhale really big? Sort of like taking in a big hot breath."

Long thought about it for a minute or two then began huffing and a puffing, blowing on the smoldering ember until it grew very red and very hot indeed. Finally, he inhaled in and out so big it blew Bo's shirt right up over his head! A few seconds later, Long began coughing and sputtering and twitching his big, spikey tail back and forth whacking off several of the smaller old stones on the bridge's walls.

"What's wrong?" cried Bo nervously.

"Too much smoke. Not working," Long choked out in a hoarse whisper, barely getting the words out as he gasped for air.

*"I'm so sorry. Oh, I'm so very sorry! But wait, I've got a better idea! Why don't you try eating a sort of burning ember sandwich but **padded** this time?"* offered Bo. *"We can make it cooler by cutting off the leafy tops of bushes and young little trees for padding. They'll act like the lettuce on a sandwich but with my hot coal in the middle. Then, when you're ready, just wolf it right down the 'ol gizzle! The green leafy stuff should take the burn out long enough for you to swallow it okay this time."*

After they'd collected all the fixings Long trustingly opened his large mouth a second time and let Bo carefully place their hot coal sandwich inside.

"Crunch, crunch, crunch," went the big teeth followed by a gigantic *"gulp."*

What felt like forever, they had waited only a few seconds or so when Long's eyes began bulging real big like they might pop right out of his head! He stood up on the end of his dragon-sized tiptoes, opened his mouth as far as it could go and shrieked *"Waaaaateeerrrr!"*

Bo ran to the river's edge as fast as his legs could carry him. He filled up his pail and sprinted back to the suffering giant throwing the water into Long's mouth. He motioned to Long to follow him back down to the river all the way. Long wasted no time and began running full out to get to it. He plunged right in and disappeared under the water completely.

Bo watched the swirling circle of bubbles remaining at the spot where Long sank into the water and noticed how more and more bubbles soon began coming up to the surface. Suddenly a great stream of water and air came blowing and squirting up out of the water as if a big elephant lay hidden below. Long surfaced next and managed to sputter out hoarsely, *"My mouth and tongue and throat are so scorched I need to stay in the water for a while to cool myself down some more. Don't worry, I heal rather quickly."*

"What are we gonna do? How can we get your fire back without burning you up first?" Bo moaned.

The two of them sat there, one in the water, one on the bank. They did some pretty serious thinking about Long's dilemma for a good, long while. Then Bo got up and announced rather triumphantly, *"I think I know how we can do this. What we need is **cool** light, a fire that's not hot, but works like fire—cool fire. **Fireflies**! They don't call them fireflies for nothing, you know!"*

"Oh, you mean lightning bugs. That's what we call them where I come from," Long sputtered out.

*"Well, technically, lighting bugs aren't even **bugs**,"* Bo stated.

"Ok, well, fireflies aren't flies either!" Long snapped back.

"I know," Bo replied, *"They're really **beetles** for heaven's sake but who cares? Their "fire" lights up. It's cool light, not hot. I think this just might work, Long!"*

For many evenings following, Bo and Long collected the little bugs—the fireflies. Finally, after Long had eaten hundreds of the little insects, a magical and wonderful thing started happening. Each time Long would go to speak, a little bit of fire escaped, fluttering out the sides of his mouth.

Bo noticed and said to Long, *"I think it's time now for you to try a full dragon roar and see if your fire has been re-lighted, safely this time. Be brave. Just go ahead and let her rip, dude!'*

Long cocked his head a little and raised his eyes wondering what Bo had meant by the words *"rip"* and *"dude"* but decided it was likely just the weird way Bo phrased things sometimes and all okay by him.

That's pretty much how it all happened. The mighty dragon roared an impressive roar with great, glorious red and golden flames pouring out of his mouth and the boy and the dragon sat there together and laughed and laughed. Their laughter came filled with nervous relief, surprise, and joy all at the same time. And it was good.

After a while, though, Long and the boy said their sweet and sad goodbyes. The big animal swam away in the river for some time and then could be seen flying high in the sky before going out of sight, returning to his own far away land where he could roar with pride among the other dragons once again. He never forgot the kind young boy who'd helped him in a most unusual way.

As for Bo, you might ask? Well, he continued to dream his dreams and listen to the animals. And whenever he looked up into the night sky, he'd find the stars in the dragon shape and he'd smile and say:

"*Don't be **long** before you come again!*"

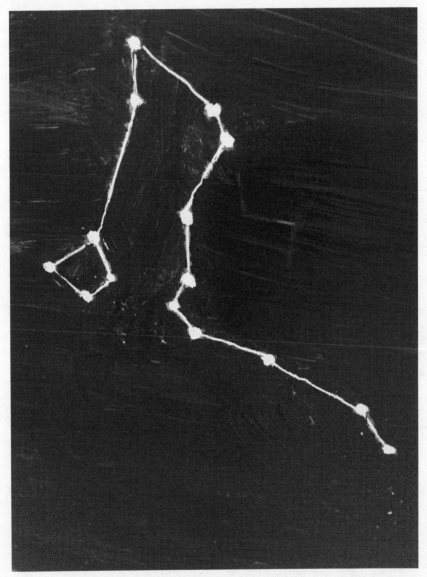

"DRACO," THE CONSTELLATION

Juicy Animal Facts From Tale Three: *The Boy and the Dragon*

"Fire Lizards"—were unproven, mythological creatures; however, some beetles have been known to spit acidic, boiling like venom and electric eels emit a shock. A huge, extinct, prehistoric giant monitor lizard called *Megalania* roamed from Asia to Australia during the Pleistocene Era thousands of years ago. Megalania's 30-foot long body was armed with razor sharp claws and teeth and deadly acidic venom it used to kill its prey—perhaps this creature was the origin of dragon tales.

Fireflies/Lightning Bugs—are the common names for a group of harmless, non-stinging and non-biting beetles that fly in the evenings during summer in the southern/eastern climates. They emit a cool light caused by the reaction of two chemical enzymes within their bodies, *luciferin* and *luciferase*.

Dragon Star—"Draco" is the name of the ancient constellation of stars seen in the northern hemisphere sky forming the outline of a dragon.

TALE FOUR

CHARLES BRONSON AND THE CROWS

The old tortoise cleared his throat signaling to his young rider he was about to begin another one of his stories. Taking the cue, Sally Scott wasted no time asking him, "Is this next story from the olden days or is it in my time?" Ezra answered her this way, "As amazing as it is, this story is quite true and most definitely from your time."

He stood there, shaking and alone. His baby bird body shivered in terror as the big crows swooped in on him pecking ferociously and squawking all the while trying to access a vulnerable spot on his young body and quickly end the struggle. But he hopped, ducked, and moved his bony stubs of tiny wings a little this way and a little that way, thrusting his little bird

CROWS ATTACK BABY BIRD

breast way out as if he was the biggest, baddest bird ever.

Every so often during the attack his memory flashed back to the roaring of the sudden terrible storm the night before as his bird family slept—he and his brother, sister, and his mother and father. Before they fully awakened, the wind had blown everything and everybody clean out of their nest in the tall treetop.

The next thing he knew he lay on the ground alone and cowering, trying to keep out of the pounding rain as best he could. When daylight finally peeked through the clouds, it hadn't taken long before the neighborhood gang of crows called *the murder* discovered him and the battle had ensued.

But now he felt his strength leaving him like a slow leak. The crow bullies appeared single-mindedly determined to wear him down. And they were so horribly loud about it too.

Right at the moment when the little bird thought he could go on no longer, a really weird thing happened—the crows suddenly flew away abandoning him completely. He didn't even have enough strength left to raise his head up to take a good look. His eyes closed gently. *"If I could just rest my eyes a second or two,"* he thought to himself.

But his little bird eyes didn't stay closed for long because he recognized an unmistakable sound and it grew closer. As young as he was he knew the distinct sound of human. He began obsessing on that scary thought when suddenly a giant scooped him up and carried him away. Again, he didn't struggle. All the fight had left him and he easily gave way to the sleepies for good this time.

When he awakened, he found himself in a small box with soft material on the bottom. It felt really good. A light shined down on him and made everything all warm and comfy. It didn't feel like he was outdoors. Somehow, though, it felt strangely okay to be just where he was.

His giant returned. The human seemed to be trying to communicate with him somehow. *"How weird,"* he thought. The human had long, light colored hair piled on top of its head. The little bird thought it looked a lot like his old bird's nest, a most pleasant thought indeed.

The human also possessed a very large mouth with big teeth. A bumped-up, squishy padding surrounded the mouth hole opening. It looked odd not having a beak like he had. As the human tried to communicate, its mouth opened and closed and the squishy padding made all kinds of shapes. All in all, the human appeared fairly pathetic to him, but oddly enough, not the least bit scary.

After a while the little blackbird strongly felt the hungries coming over him. Birds eat often and baby birds eat even more frequently. He wondered, *"Maybe it was all the crow fighting. Maybe it worked up a fierce appetite in me?"* But no usual mixture of seeds or other good stuff came for him from his mother or father bird this time. It didn't take long before the little bird could hear himself crying out,

"Peep, peep. Peep, peep#*!" That's bird speak for *"Heeeelllp! I'm starving here!"*

The human listened to his pitiful cries and began working hard to find some food suitable for him. She didn't know what a suitable food for a baby bird might be. It wasn't every day she had a baby blackbird as a houseguest. She didn't even know what kind of blackbird he was exactly.

The human mixed some things together she'd read blackbirds commonly ate in the spring. Then she smiled her big puffy mouth as she tenderly offered the food to the little bird who gulped it all down immediately. The human then made some movements and sounds with her huge mouth and said, *"I'm naming you Charles Bronson because you are a very brave little bird who never gave up fighting for his life."* The human chose the name *Charles Bronson* for her new bird friend from a popular old movie star, a male human who'd had that name and was tough as nails in a very cool way.

The baby bird Charles Bronson soon understood the human meant to help him. He had no need to fear it. And a most peculiar friendship began to grow between the bird and the kind human, a lady named Melinda.

As time went by and much to Melinda's surprise, Charles Bronson grew and seemed happy and safe in his new life with her and her black and white dog, Lily.

At some point, Melinda noticed a yellow circle growing around each of the bird's eyes. This distinctive trait helped her discover what kind of blackbird he was. Charles Bronson was a *grackle*, a distant cousin to a crow but more the size of a robin and a lot more handsome Melinda thought.

Melinda talked to Charles Bronson and soothed him with soft sounds of her voice. She encouraged him to exercise his little budding wings up and down, up and down. She helped him take little birdbaths so he'd be clean and feel better. Charles Bronson really, really liked his baths!

Melinda searched for ideas to help her make interesting little food treats Charles Bronson might enjoy eating. She discovered a big food hit when Charles Bronson tried watermelon for the first time. He knew his life would never be the same for he had not known anything tasting quite so sweet.

Every time Melinda came to the bird's little box she said his name, *"Charles Bronson, good morning,"* or *"Hi there, Charles Bronson!"* Amazingly, it didn't take long before Charles Bronson knew exactly who Charles Bronson was, and this is the honest truth.

Now what's even more interesting in this wonderfully true story is when you compare Charles Bronson's new life with the way grackles naturally live and how they normally behave. For example, grackles in the wild grow up with a clear fear of humans and their human pets … like dogs, for instance. But in Charles Bronson's case, he loved the human's dog too. And Melinda's dog loved him back. There simply was nothing ordinary about the little bird's new life—nothing ordinary whatsoever.

Every time Lily dog tried to kiss the little bird on the tip of his beak, Charles Bronson would try his hardest not to steal a little love peck from the dog's tender tongue. The bond between the dog and the grackle grew as strong and extraordinary as the one growing between Melinda and Charles Bronson.

Trust between Lily and the bird grew through lots of game playing, too. For example, Charles Bronson teased Lily by tickling the dog with the tip of his beak on the soft pads under her feet while she tried to take a nap. Or better still, Charles Bronson perched on the edge of Lily's green food bowl sometimes and tried to spear little tasty morsels the dog seemed to be ignoring.

The bird simply enjoyed his life fully. He loved jabbing his awesome beak into chunks of food and feeling the power of it. He also adored it when Lily took him for little rides on her back. Lily enjoyed it all, too, like she had a special little play buddy.

All the while Charles Bronson grew and played and bonded with his human and dog pals, the same sinister group of seven crows who had attacked Charles Bronson when he was just a baby had been watching from a distance.

Most of the time the crows performed their vigilant black watch hidden high above in the dark shadows of

Charles Bronson and Lily Kiss

nearby granddaddy pine trees. Only their eyes peering out could be seen if anyone had been looking their way.

As they watched and waited, they also wondered. They wondered what in the world a grackle bird was doing paling around with a human and a dog and living with them in their house for heaven's sakes!

They were patient, those crows, strategic really, as they waited. They looked for the perfect opportunity, not just any old opportunity, but the perfect one to success-fully land them a grackle dinner. They kept unusually quiet while they watched—didn't want anyone to notice them.

As protected as Charles Bronson lived in those days with his human and dog friends, he'd find out on one clear sunny morning how unprepared he actually had been. Unexpectedly, in just a flash of a moment, the lone crow on watch duty saw the human and dog nowhere in sight and Charles Bronson outside all alone on the back-yard deck. Charles Bronson strolled around unaware on Melinda's glass top table with the umbrella fully opened from the pole extending through the hole in the middle of the table.

The crow screamed out a dreadful piercing sig-nal to all his murder pals and literally in seconds the ever-watching crow gang had all quietly assembled on Melinda's deck fence. As soon as all the crows took their places on the wooden fence, they began to squawk and carry on loudly. They'd caught Charles Bronson off guard and they knew it.

SALLY SCOTT GUYNN

A MURDER OF CROWS WAIT

And then, slowly at first, one by one they began taking turns zooming in to try and land a peck at the now fully aware grackle. He bobbed and weaved impressively, putting up a brave and athletic defense. After several minutes, though, he could already feel his energy slowly threatening to leave him. The crows sensed his slowing and in unison increased the volume of their taunts and the force of their attacks.

All this commotion eventually got the attention of the grackle's pal Lily dog who by luck Melinda had just let outside. Lily came bounding around to the rear of the house and jumped smack dab right into the middle of the fray without hesitation. She barked and leaped and snapped at the obsessive crows.

At one point Lily moved close by the edge of the table and Charles Bronson just gently hopped off the table and onto the dog's back! He held onto Lily's long fur as tightly as he could with his now almost grown-up big bird feet.

Lily peeked her head around to be certain of what had just happened, and then she upped the tempo of her defensive moves at the crows. It was as if she'd suddenly been empowered by Charles Bronson's arrival on her back.

The spectacle continued like the dog-gonest thing you ever saw. Without saying anything, both animals understood working together as a team. Lily went into super-drive and nipped at the crows, pulled tail feathers out, jumped up in the air barking ferociously, flung one or two of them through the air, all the while Charles Bronson cheering her on with his rough, grackley bird sounds. They weren't pretty sounds for sure but they added to the drama nicely.

After a while, the crows knew they'd been beaten. They gave up and flew away and stayed away. And that was that. Charles Bronson and Lily felt very proud of themselves and each other.

Once Charles Bronson had fully matured, the day finally arrived when Melinda knew the time had come for her to release him back into the wild from where he'd come. She feared for him since he'd only known a human and a dog.

She worried his knowing only how to live inside would make it more challenging for him outside in the wilds. Had he grown up outside he would've learned how to contend with the normal pressures in nature like finding food and shelter, fending off enemies, competing with other grackles for a mate, foul weather and so forth.

But Melinda suspected Charles Bronson's destiny laid in greater things than he'd experienced so far with her. Letting him go free was simply the right thing to do, but its being right didn't make Melinda any less scared for him or her heart any less sad.

One beautiful morning Melinda took Charles Bronson outside to her deck where he went every day with her. He'd typically sit there on her shoulder while she enjoyed her morning coffee. But on this particular morning

Melinda released Charles Bronson from her hand up into the air with a single fling of her arm and a firm command, *"Fly Charles Bronson. Fly."* And so he did, zooming off into the air like a pro.

Melinda found herself unprepared for what she discovered the next day when she walked out onto her deck. Charles Bronson came flying in to her like a jet plane approaching the runway. He flew straight to her for their morning ritual just like he had an appointment to keep. Later, he flew back to his outside place, wherever that was, close by most likely, and spent the night.

The next morning he returned, and the next, and the next morning after that. To this day, Charles Bronson flies in every morning keeping his appointment to check in with his beloved human friend, Melinda, and his pal, Lily. Even more remarkable is if Melinda goes out to her deck at anytime during the day and calls Charles Bronson by name, he comes quickly flying right back to her. It's as if he just sits in a tree somewhere close by and waits for her to call him.

At this point in Ezra's storytelling, the old tortoise swore the story of Charles Bronson was a true one and added a few facts about the kind of grackle bird he was. Because Ezra had seen them for real in the wild he knew grackles preferred to be in the company of large groups of their kind. When they grouped together they were known as a plague of grackles.

On his own, Charles Bronson learned quickly how big groups of grackles also included other types of black-birds sometimes. When they stopped to sit in tall trees together in large numbers of dozens, hundreds, or even thousands of blackbirds, they all felt much safer from predators trying to catch them for dinner.

And so it was for Charles Bronson after his release back into the wild—not the same as living in the house with Melinda and her dog, but a mighty fine second. Charles Bronson hangs out now with his gang, the *plague,* when he's not with his human and dog pals. Not surprisingly, he's never had any trouble with the crows again.

To this day Charles Bronson can be seen looking most dashing as he strikes a pose most mornings sitting on the very top of the roof of Melinda's house or on a tall tree close by. He looks every bit the brave guard bird he's become. And he looks happy.

A GROWN-UP CHARLES BRONSON LISTENS FOR MELINDA'S VOICE

JUICY ANIMAL FACTS FROM TALE FOUR:
CHARLES BRONSON AND THE CROWS

Crows—are large, black and very smart birds common in America and other parts of the world. They are closely related to ravens and magpies; a bunch of crows that live together are called a *"murder"*. Crows are smaller than but look similar to ravens in the western United States.

Blackbirds—are a common name for grackles, cowbirds, and starlings, none of which are songbirds. The grackle's voice is raspy, not pretty; some blackbirds can be seen migrating over a city in huge groups in the morning and then back to where they roost, or sleep, in the evening.

Grackles—are not solidly black in color. They commonly eat grains, sunflower seeds, corn, acorns, and some fruits. They may also gobble up goldfish, minnows, crayfish, small frogs, baby house sparrows, mice and small bats they catch in the air.

THE THREE LITTLE CADDISFLIES

Ezra began telling his fifth tale to Sally Scott by first letting her know this tale would be about very unlikely animals, perhaps animals she'd never even heard of before. With her curiosity once again aroused, Sally Scott promised to give the old tortoise her fullest attention, so Ezra began.

Once, not so long ago in a rocky, narrow, cold mountain stream there lived three little caddisfly larvae. Actually insect brothers, they lived completely under the stream's swiftly flowing waters, a mostly happy arrangement.

The youngest caddisfly, Dritus, basically had a big dose of the lazies. Not surprising, his favorite thing was napping and feeling the cool water flow over him.

The middle brother, named Twix, mostly enjoyed playing pranks and kidding around. He just couldn't get too serious about anything. He especially loved experimenting with his special, sticky caddisfly saliva, or *spittle*. It acted like a strong glue, and he could always find something really cool to stick somewhere with his awesome spittle.

The oldest of the three brothers, Peb, was clearly of the serious sort. He worried about this and that and preferred making plans so he'd always be prepared. His brothers thought him a little too bossy.

Interestingly, these little caddisflies weren't exactly caddis*flies* yet. As a matter of fact they weren't flies at all. Technically they were caddisfly *larvae*—wormy looking little guys about a half inch or so long and looking a lot like a really small caterpillar, except in the water rather than on land.

Dritus, Twix and Peb lived an *aquatic* life as larvae, totally under the water. Since the brothers hadn't grown up yet, they were somewhat like human children in that they were adults in-the-making, so to speak. But in the insect world there simply would be no parents to care for them and no one to protect them. It's just the way it worked.

The brothers mostly busied themselves scraping off stuff stuck to rocks or eating small particles of food floating by them in the currents of the water. And just like a butterfly caterpillar or a moth in its cocoon, the three brothers lived unaware, clueless how their lives would change one day when they became full-grown adult caddisflies.

One day, that is, if they played it real clever-like and their luck held out so they could outsmart and outswim their archenemy, Trebor. The pointy-clawed, crusty old crayfish Trebor lived in the same stream, lurking ominously about when not hiding among the rocks there. Trebor's skulking around wasn't aimless wandering either. He possessed an insatiable appetite with a razor-sharp focus on finding food.

To the little caddisfly larvae, Trebor at four times their size looked like a humongous monster with eight clawed legs, sinister protruding eyes and two awful pinchers capable of ripping apart a larvae's body in the wink of an eye! As you might guess, the caddisflies and other small critters living in the stream greatly feared Trebor.

If the way Trebor looked wasn't menacing enough to scare the willikers out of the brothers, there were always his awful sounds to complete the terror. As a true predator in pursuit of his next meal, Trebor relentlessly hunted, and while he hunted his body clanked noisily into the pebbles and other debris in the stream creating loud echoing sounds and scary underwater reverberations.

As in all crayfish, Trebor had a hard, outside body covering. Instead of soft skin, he had an *exoskeleton*, sort of like a crustacean wearing knight of the round-table armor but actually part of his body. While it protected him very well, the clanking noises complicated Trebor's hunting since the sounds announced his nearing presence and gave his prey some time to make their escape.

ARCHENEMY, TREBOR THE CRAYFISH

The brothers well knew they must protect themselves from the horrible Trebor. As you might imagine, big brother Peb, the nerdiest of the three, began planning early on just how he'd build his caddisfly case home. Like all caddisfly *"houses,"* his case would have an entrance just big enough for him to crawl in and then he'd actually carry it around him to keep him safe. He'd be sort of like a hermit crab inside a shell he carries around except Peb would be able to spit his gluey spittle onto rock surfaces as needed.

Peb's ultimate plan focused on building his case home absolutely as strong as possible. He decided to build his entirely out of little pebbles he'd glue together. But first he wisely chose a big flat rock on the stream's bottom to build his case home on. He thought the flat rock might also make an ideal space to share with his two brothers when they completed their case homes.

Before doing any actual work himself, young Dritus boasted in a loud, rhyming sort of rap verse how his case home would be THE BEST ever:

"I'm building my case out of leaves.
They'll stick together if you please,
Mud and spit the things I'll use,
Plenty of time to catch a snooze. Ha,Ha, Ha!" Once he finished boasting, Dritus collected a few pieces of leaves but soon grew bored and went off to take a nap.

Not long after hearing Dritus, middle brother Twix couldn't help himself and vainly proclaimed how great his case home would be. *"I'm building **my** case out of* *twigs,*" he yelled out. Then not to be outdone by Dritus he thought for a moment or two and added in rap:

"Twigs and sticks are stronger than leaves,
So I'll gather wood pieces floating from trees;
I'll scrape them from the bottom of this fast flowing stream,
*It won't take long to build **my** dream;*
I'll glue it together with mud and spittle,
I'll build it on Peb's rock right in the middle."

For a while at least, Twix worked on his little fort-like case according to his plan, but soon he, like Dritus, lost interest and started making excuses:

"Life's too short to waste my day,
Hunting for sticks when I'd rather play;
I've got plenty already, I dare say,
To work any more just a big nay-nay!" And Twix wiggled off merrily to play.

For many months big brother Peb visited his two brothers who lived within earshot. He worried greatly for them because they still hadn't built their cases as sturdy as they should've been. He tried warning Dritus over and over: *"Better add more leaves, mud and spittle; a lot more spit will sure help a little!"* Peb always added gentle advice with his warnings. *"Better to be safe than sorry, bro!"* he'd say.

Dritus still just laughed him off and yelled back playfully in rapping verse:

"I'll finish this project quick as a wink,

Just a dab of mud is all I think,
It oughta be enough, I wanna go play;
Got better things to do, it's a beautiful day." And off
Dritus went.

Peb also tried to warn Twix, saying: *"Better add more*
twig pieces to that case of yours; maybe add more spit glue
to harden'em like boards!"

Every time he tried to warn Twix, just like Dritus,
he'd hardly get the words out when Twix would begin to
laugh and laugh, saying, *"You're just a 'Nervous Nelly',*
Peb; go get a life now instead!"

So many months of futile attempts to warn his brothers had frustrated Peb. But what could he do? He always
left them shaking his head and frowning as he hurried
away to continue strengthening his own house. While
he crawled along he talked out loud to himself, saying:

"I'll keep building on my case house so it'll be strong;
I'm finding the pebbles, it won't take long;
I'll glue them and stack them every one,
If danger comes I won't have to run!"

With his usual grit, Peb worked and worked, gathering many little pebbles and fashioning them into a tightly
built dwelling to go around his body. Using his spittle,
he attached his case lightly to the rock he'd chosen in
the fast-moving stream. He attached it lightly so he'd be
able to break it loose when he needed to crawl about and
find food. Every day he surveyed his work and reassured
himself, saying with confidence, *"This house is good; I've*
made it strong; now I can rest where I belong."

DRITUS' CASE HOUSE OF LEAF BITS

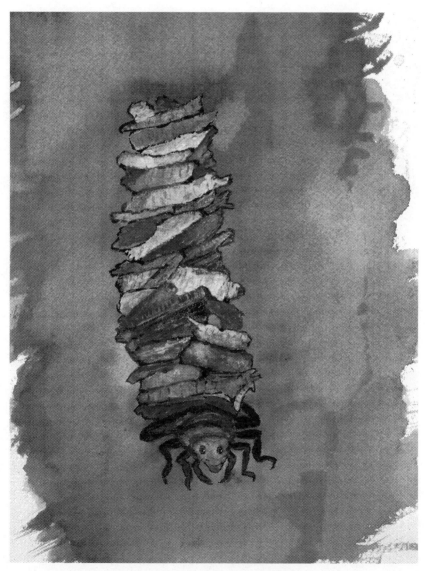

TWIX' CASE HOUSE OF TWIG PIECES

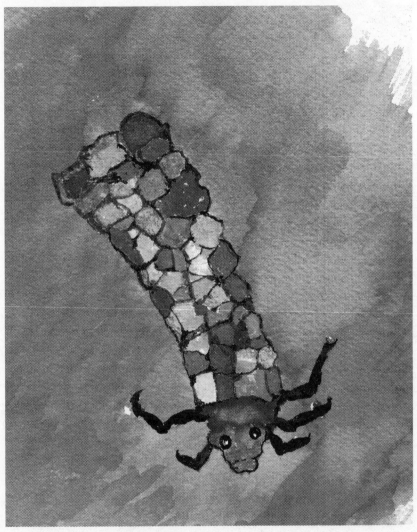

PEB'S CASE HOUSE OF PEBBLES

Many months later, the caddisfly brothers grouped together one evening and soon began to argue about who had built the best case for their house. As they argued, their voices grew louder and louder, each one boasting as to the merits of their excellent building skills.

Young Dritus got so worked up he foolishly yelled a challenge to Trebor as loudly as he could out into the watery darkness of the night:

"You'll never get me, Trebor you meanie,

My case around me is leaf-built though teenie;

But you'll never get me, no sir-reenie! Ha, ha, ha!"

In truth, Trebor didn't actually try to be mean. He was simply being himself, doing his thing. He couldn't choose not to be a predator. He was what he was and it was as natural as the grass is green.

And Trebor did not lack any when it came to his own set of problems living in the wild. You see, while he lived and breathed in the water his entire life, tirelessly searching for caddisfly larvae, worms, frog eggs, snails or whatever he might happen upon, he, too, faced challenges on occasion.

One of Trebor's challenges in particular deserves mentioning. As the crayfish aged, every so often he literally would outgrow his own body. At that time he became weak and inactive sort of like feeling a little sick. But then he'd actually shed his outer body shell once he'd grown a new, bigger one underneath. When the outer shell came off, the new one below it remained soft for a short time until it hardened and that made the already weakened Trebor easy prey for a bigger animal on the prowl.

While still visiting at Peb's, Twix piped up after Dritus to boast again about his handiwork, too. He didn't want to be outdone by his younger brother so he began bragging loudly about his case house and then he, too, began yelling out an even louder challenge to Trebor:

"You'll not get me you crabby old crayfish,
No matter how much you might fret, yell or wish;
I built my house out of sticks and spit,
No cause for you to throw a fit;
So chill your hunt fever you freaky gill breather!"

Now here's the thing. All the while they yelled and boasted to each other underwater, none of them realized how the sound of their voices carried more easily through the water and smack dab right to the hearing of Trebor himself. He just silently smiled a weird, wicked smile that slowly spread across his entire crusty face.

The next day each of the three little caddisfly larvae in their separate case houses awakened to the dreaded sounds of eight mighty crayfish legs, one by one clanging against the rocks in the stream and making the most fearsome noise ever.

"Boom, boom, boom, boom, boom, boom, boom, boom!"

"Run for your life!" Dritus cried out as loudly as he could, barely escaping the giant crayfish as Trebor came crashing loudly through his case house. Only one stroke

THE BROTHERS IN THEIR HOUSES ON ROCKY STREAM BOTTOM

of his mighty armored claw left Dritus' home of leaves pretty much trashed.

Dritus arrived at brother Twix's house in the nick of time to warn him, screaming, *"Get out, get out! Too late to knock! Trebor's come for you now, he's at our big rock!"* So the two larvae quickly fled toward older brother Peb's case house of pebbles.

Moments later they heard the sounds of a huge crayfish tailfin crashing through Twix's nearby stick house, mashing it flat as a pancake! The stream's flowing water had carried the two brothers along easily over the big rock to Peb's house, but it didn't lessen the panic and confusion they felt growing inside them.

The younger brothers arrived at Peb's just moments before each of their bodies began to tense up strangely. It felt like their skin tightened then hardened all over. Finally, the hardened skin enclosed Twix completely within a small dark, mummy-like capsule. He slid gently over the side of the big rock where his house had been attached. It remained there stuck to the edge of the rock's underside. Moments later the very same thing happened to Dritus.

Try as he might, Trebor could not find the two brothers.

When Peb fearfully stole a peek out of his case home to see how close Trebor was, he could no longer see his brothers on top of the rock. But before he could go look for them he, too, began to feel strange changes within his body. The pressure increased until he finally had to sneak out of his house while the same kind of hardened encasement formed very quickly around him.

Unnoticed by Trebor, Peb crawled slowly away from his old house of pebbles and clung with his brothers, all in their new mummy-like cases, to the underside of the rock. Exhausted, Trebor clanked away to find food elsewhere.

Over the next few days all three brothers felt strange changes continuing to happen in their bodies. Then Trebor's familiar, terrifyingly awful noise in the distance could be heard. It grew louder and louder as he came closer and closer still. Finally, he thundered through the water circling the big rock around and around while sending watery shock waves out in every direction as he desperately searched for the brothers.

In their separate encasements the three brothers huddled, shaking in fear as they listened to the now close-up sounds of giant claws grating against the outside walls of Peb's sturdy but now empty pebble house on the rock above.

Trebor attacked over and over with all his force. They could hear his body armor crashing about as he thrashed his tail this way and that, back and forth, rattling the very foundation of Peb's house. But the little house stood firm.

Try as he might, Trebor could not move those pebbles. He caused only minimal damage to Peb's house, not enough to destroy it altogether. But he wouldn't leave the house alone either and continued to storm it, driven by the thought of having tasty caddisfly for dinner.

Trebor left the scene every now and then, most likely to eat, but he'd return to continue his siege. The crayfish's frustration grew as he obsessed with destroying Peb's house. He didn't even notice when the brothers in their hard covered, darkened bodies left the rock's underside and began swimming with great effort up to the waters' surface.

There an amazing thing began to take place as they floated along. At first, all three brothers thought things seemed a little strange because they'd been scared out of their wits, but soon they realized something else must be happening to them as they struggled with all their might against the current near the stream's surface.

One by one, first Peb, then Twix, and finally Dritus all felt a growing pressure under their skin, then a strong tightening in their little bodies all over. It felt odd, all tingly and strange, but it didn't hurt. And then, slowly, and just as natural as could be, each one of their entire body's hard outer covering simply fell off like an old coat!

Their new caddisfly bodies looked and felt different—wonderfully different! Gone were their former wormy looks and gone were their mummy-encased bodies, replaced now with six long slender legs each and graceful pointed feet. Their new bodies were shapely too, and then, most importantly, each brother had their own pair of wings!

They simply could not be more amazed at themselves! *"We have wings!"* they shouted. Having wings had to be the absolutely most coolest thing ever! They began struggling hard to flutter them. They could still partially hear Trebor freaking out in the water below them as he continued trying to destroy Peb's house. Luckily, the dastardly crayfish remained oblivious to the brothers' absence below and their now floating downstream on the currents' surface.

Finally, their wing-flapping efforts paid off. All three of the brothers felt the power of their new wings awaken and propel them fairly effortlessly from the water completely. In just seconds they found themselves air born, flying in a new world filled with clean, bright, warm air. Flying felt magical.

Their big day had come at last—the biggest day of their lives—their final day of change into full-grown, adult caddisflies! No more being aqua dudes running scared from an obsessive lobster wannabe!

Their final and most dramatic life change had happened most unexpectedly and at the best, most amazing moment for them, considering Trebor so close on their trails. Just like that the three little caddisflies had been reborn and Trebor in an instant merely a thing of the past. While unsure of what their lives would be like from now on, they were certain of one thing—they'd never again shirk their responsibilities or foolishly taunt another living being!

BECOMING ADULTS

JUICY ANIMAL FACTS FROM TALE FIVE: THE THREE LITTLE CADDISFLIES

Caddisfly larvae—are insects that live part of their life as immature larvae in cold, fast-flowing freshwater streams usually attached to rocks on the bottom of the streams in small cases they construct from bits of leaves, twigs, small pebbles, or a combination. Since they can only survive by living in clean water, scientists use them as *bio-indicators* of the health or purity of the stream like canaries in a coal mine.

Caddisfly spittle—is their special saliva they use to cement the pebbles, twigs or leaves together into the cases for shelter and to cement themselves to a rock so they won't be swept away while they feed.

Flies—are a type of insect we commonly think of as houseflies. They are air-breathing, flying insects that never live in water and they are different from the caddisflies featured in this story.

Aquatic—is the name describing either a stage or the entire span of an animal's life that is lived entirely in water, for example, fish are aquatic animals.

Cocoon—is a type of case the larvae of immature moths spin out of silk to protect them until they leave the case as adult moths with wings.

Crayfish—are freshwater crustaceans similar to, but smaller than lobsters. Crayfish live in freshwater streams or brackish water in some places. Lobsters live only in marine, or saltwater.

Exoskeleton—is the hard, outer covering of some insects and crustaceans that they must shed (called *molting*) every so often so the animal can grow bigger in size.

Caddisfly House—the small encasements caddisfly larvae build for protection out of twigs, leaves, pebbles or a combination and then crawl into them, carrying them around and attaching them lightly to rocks in freshwater streams when they don't need mobility.

Metamorphosis—is the series of changes in the bodies of some insects that they must go through to become adults. In the case of caddisflies, the changes are called *complete* metamorphosis since they first go through an egg stage, then a wormy-looking larvae stage, then in a hardened case stage as a pupa, and then finally changing one last time into quite a different looking adult caddisfly leaving the water flying and breathing air.

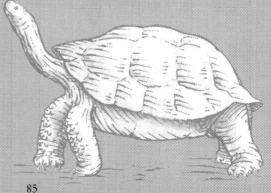

TALE SIX

STINKY–THE GOAT WHO WOULD BE COW

Ezra began telling another tale, but this time his voice had softened almost to a whisper when he communicated to Sally Scott saying, "What you are about to hear is a true story with almost no embellishments." He paused for a moment as if he were thinking back and remembering, and then he began Tale Six.

The night was so cold and scary dark that the little baby goat's teeth chattered uncontrollably. He tried to make a bleating goat sound but nothing came out. The truck jiggled and rocked along, making him feel sleepy in spite of the cold. Finally, he stopped wiggling and just relaxed into the rocking of the truck and the warmth of the towel the human had wrapped around him.

The truck pulled into what smelled and looked like a human's place. He couldn't see all the way out of the truck's fogged-up back window, making it hard to tell. The wind had picked up and sleet began spitting down when the human in the front seat suddenly reached back and picked him up, towel and all, just after the truck jerked to a full stop.

"*Whaaat?*" the little goat bleated out sleepily. "*Baaaaaaaa?*" he bleated out again with all his might. He couldn't figure out exactly what was happening, but he sensed his life was about to change–a lot. Holding the baby goat under one arm, the human opened the truck door and stepped out into the inky dark night.

When they reached the farmhouse, the door opened before them and a human they called Marty Putz greeted them warmly. She held a baby calf in her arms while nursing him from a weird looking bottle of milk. The little calf appeared to be quite comfortable and paid them no mind whatsoever.

Marty sat down in a well-worn rocking chair, still holding the nursing calf when her husband, Bob, wearing bib overalls, entered the room. Bob looked at his wife, then the calf, and finally the little goat. Then he smiled, well sort of smiled anyway. He and the human from the truck left the room and Marty tucked the little goat into an open cardboard box with a clean towel in it. The goat closed his eyes, then sighed a long sigh and gave-in to the heaviness of his eyelids.

The next day the weather had improved greatly. Early in the morning Farmer Marty walked to her kitchen and put a small log on the warming fire in the big stone fireplace. Next, she peeked into the cardboard box nearby with the towel and the baby goat still sleeping inside. She took a deep breath and began to size up the baby, muttering out loud to herself, *"Now let's take a good look at ya … find out what we got here."*

Farmer Marty saw a very young male, probably only several weeks old. He was all white and adorably cute. She scooped the baby goat up into her arms and then walked over to a second cardboard box and picked up the little calf from the night before. She plopped down in her rocker holding both the slowly awakening babies, one under each arm. She grabbed two weird bottles of milk from a little table next to the rocking chair and began feeding both the animals. The babies eagerly gulped down the milk and then rested like all was perfectly normal.

The little calf's mother had not been able to give milk to her baby and Farmer Marty had taken over the job for her. The little goat's mother died at his birth, and the goat farmer and his wife were too old to take care of an orphaned baby goat. The goat farmer brought the little goat to Marty because most everyone in the Shepherdstown highlands there knew of her kindnesses to animals and her willingness to take in animals in need of care. Along with about fourteen cows, Farmers Marty and Bob had a few sheep, some fancy looking chickens, and several cats who roamed freely on their farm with a small band of cocky peacocks.

As the days rolled by into spring, the two baby animals grew stronger and bigger just like their friendship. When they outgrew their boxes in the kitchen, Farmer Marty turned them out into the pasture with the rest of the cows and their calves.

Part of the pasture sloped down. It made a perfect raceway for a young goat and a young calf to experiment with how fast they could go. They practiced zooming down it as fast as their legs could carry them. When the young goat couldn't resist the urge any longer, he reverted to rolling down the hill instead.

Although they received many dirty looks from the adult cows whenever they ran around in the pasture like aliens from outer space, the two young friends agreed it was well worth the disdain they received. Sometimes they pretended to wrestle and push each other around, but quickly nuzzled to make sure the other was okay. They got a kick out of making the weirdest noises too. But their most favorite thing of all remained butting their heads and pretending to be great bulls or wild mountain goats.

Eventually, the Putz farmers named the young calf "Four" since he was the fourth calf born on their farm that season. His reddish brown color and white blazed face matched the other cows in the field but he always stood out to the little goat because he was his best friend.

It didn't take long before Farmers Bob and Marty could see how close Four and the goat had become. The two young animals ran around chasing each other and finding all kinds of mischief to get into and pranks to pull on the other cows who acted pretty stuck up if the truth be known. Soon the calf and the goat became practically inseparable.

The farmer couple also noticed a few particularly worrisome things about the little goat. For one thing, besides Four, he didn't seem to be able to befriend himself to any of the other cows. They walked away from him as soon as he approached them.

And when the mother cows put all the calves together on the edge of the pasture for a while, as usual, so the mothers could graze without interruption, the farmers noticed another problem. Every time the little goat tried to join the other calves in their little "calf nursery" for the day, the adult cow on nursery duty promptly ushered him out. Only after he'd tried over and over to sneak in and nap with the other calves could he wear down the resolve of the cow on nursery duty. Even then, she'd insist on Stinky napping way over on the farthest edge of the little circle of napping calves. The little goat thought about this injustice a lot.

"I just want to be included with the others. No biggie. I really don't even need to nap as much as the calves seem to. I wanna play more. If it weren't for Four, I probably wouldn't get to play at all. I think these cows are just too serious about, about, uh … well just about everything!" he muttered to himself in dismay.

Apparently, being unpopular wasn't the only unusual thing about the young goat. The truth of the matter, at least in part, was he had a rather obvious problem with gas. He frequently released these awful gas stink bombs causing the cows in the field to grow more disgusted with him as time went on, all, that is, except for his pal, Four. Pretty soon everyone started calling the little goat "Stinky." Even though the farmers' last name was Putz, everyone soon referred to Stinky as "Stinky Butts," not Putz.

Whenever they had a chance, the other animals teased and chanted a rap at him:

"Here comes that Stinky butts,

He's a goat and psycho nuts,

So run, stay clear, he's got power in the rear!"

Such razzing likely would've embarrassed most, but Stinky took it in stride. He didn't let it bother him too much, at least not outwardly. He felt grateful he had a home, a best friend, and a safe life. But a sadness began to grow inside his heart like a stubborn fog on a gray day.

As time passed, Stinky and Four ultimately had no choice but to begin learning the rules of being a good cow. Fortunately, the herd didn't have a huge number of rules, only five of them—five cardinal rules. As such, everyone had to obey them at all times and without fail. The strictness of the rules had to do with safety and protecting the herd. And, like it or not, Stinky was now part of a herd.

Cow Rule #1: "In the morning, you walk only in a single file line and in your proper place in the line."

Fourteen adult female cows and their calves grazed together in the Putz pasture. An older, wiser cow named Clara led them. First thing in the morning, Clara took her important position at the head of the single file lineup of cows and began walking from the barn area usually over to whatever area she chose for them to first begin grazing that day. When they'd eaten most of the grass in the first area, Clara led them over to another area to graze and so on. There was never any bickering about it either. They all just stepped in line and followed their lead cow, Clara. It was the cow way of things.

But the whole walking-in-line-and-in-order thing really frustrated Stinky. Being a goat made him naturally faster than a cow in most everything. It seemed stupid to him to waste time plodding along at the very end of the same line every morning when he could get to where he wanted to graze much faster on his own. Besides, he might not want to graze where Clara led them.

Cow Rule #2: "Unless there's danger, or you're lost or hurt, you should mostly be quiet."

Stinky didn't find it as hard to follow Cow Rule #2 as he did for Rule #1. His goat bleating simply lacked the volume of the cow's mooing. But sometimes, when he walked slowly along in his usual place literally at the very tail end of the line in the early morning on a beautiful, sunny, spring day, well, he just couldn't contain himself and he'd let out a series of *"Baaaa. Baaaa. Baaaa,"* each bleat followed by a gleeful leap high into the air.

Stinky Spontaneously Glee Jumping

Some may have asked, *"Why does he do that jumping thing?"* The answer should have been *"For no particular reason other than just because he can."* And Stinky reasoned to himself, *"No one's behind me, I'm always last, so how would anyone really know and why should they even care?"*

Cow Rule #3: "When you're in the calf nursery, you must stay there, mostly napping, or looking like you're napping until the nursery cow in charge moves all the calves together from the nursery to another part of the pasture."

Stinky learned to deal with Rule #3 by sheer will. He made himself stay with the other young ones in the calf nursery, not necessarily napping, but at least remaining in there. Because Four also stayed in the nursery it wasn't too bad a deal for Stinky to handle the forced confinement. Unlike most of the calves, however, Stinky chose to stand up most of the time or lay in the grass with his head up looking about or poked through the boards of the pasture fence. To do otherwise he found simply way too boring, and Stinky was just the kind of fella who got bored rather easily.

Cow Rule #4: "No drama—this means no kicking, biting, hard head-butting or other stuff like that."

Stinky thought this rule really was for idiots. He just couldn't envision a bunch of mostly female cows with their young running around acting crazy like that. It was SO not them. He wondered, *"Do they really need a **rule*** *for this?"* Fortunately, for the most part, his innocent play antics and goofing off with Four usually didn't count as seriously breaking the rules, their being only young-sters and all. But they wouldn't be youngsters forever.

Cow Rule #5: *"You must try to keep yourself clean."*

This last rule, for Stinky at least, struck him as totally unfair. After all, he didn't have a mother to lick the dirt off him all the time like the others in the field did. *"And besides,"* Stinky reasoned to himself, *"I'm all white for goodness sakes! They're dark reddish brown. Let's see … white … dark … which one's easier to see dirt? Ya think it might be the white one? Where's the justice in this?"*

The cows' disdain for Stinky grew no matter how hard he tried to follow all the rules all the time. The bot-tom line was he didn't **look** like a cow, he didn't **sound** like a cow, and he didn't **act** like a cow.

If those three facts weren't enough reasons for the cows to look down on him and stay away from him, three more personal issues sealed his fate. First, Stinky clearly had an identity crisis—he was a pathetic goat trying to live like a cow, for heavens sake.

Secondly, Stinky had really gross personal hygiene. In other words, he was dirty and he stank, not to mention his constant gas emissions. Even more infuriating, he didn't seem to care.

Third, Stinky didn't move slow enough or keep still long enough to measure up to basic cow standards. Overall, nothing ever seemed to be enough for him. He always looked for something different to do and remained constantly curious about non-cow kinds of things.

After four months or so, a big truck showed up mysteriously one day and two men and a dog yelled and yelled and rounded up all the calves of a certain good size and age. Most of them were grazing by then just like their mothers. They loaded them into the truck and all the calves began mooing and bawling and all their mothers began doing the same. It was awful.

The men tried without success to capture Stinky, too, and load him into the truck along with the others. But Stinky had recognized the danger almost immediately and jumped over the fence to safety. He peered out between the fence boards and watched the truck roar away with his dear Four and the other calves all still bawling as the truck disappeared from sight. Trembling, Stinky vowed never to allow a human to catch him again. Never ever.

With Four gone, Stinky felt the cows' rejection more and more. The sadness in his heart grew heavier, but he couldn't figure out what he could do, if anything, to make the cows and the rest of the calves remaining in the field act differently toward him. Then one summer day everything changed.

A warm sun and a delightful breeze had ushered in a new day quite nicely. The cows and Stinky grazed in the delicious green grass of Farmer Bob's pasture. He kept his pasture in good shape. The grass grew lush and

SALLY SCOTT GUYNN

STINKY BIDS FOUR GOODBYE

98

mostly free of pesky thorn thistles so painful to a cow's tongue if one didn't pay attention while grazing.

The nice day seemed fairly typical and everyone in the field felt pretty lazy and good in the morning sun. A little later though, Stinky noticed the birds no longer sang. Curious, he stopped chomping away on the wildflowers in his mouth and raised his head up to take a quick look around. The lovely gentle breeze had stopped completely like it hit a wall or something. The sky appeared even more troubling. It seemed to be filling up rapidly with big, black, foreboding clouds, carrying smaller white puffs within them.

"*Wind!*" Stinky thought out loud right away. "*White puffy business inside black clouds ... definitely wind coming.*"

No sooner had he predicted a weather change than the wind suddenly picked up, blowing hard through the trees at the end of the pasture. The wind gusts bent the tree limbs making them sway dramatically, and it created an awful sound like a giant train roaring through at full force. A fierce lightning bolt suddenly flashed in the sky followed by a loud, close burst of thunder.

The angry clouds wasted no time unleashing giant-sized, icy cold raindrops that felt like a million needles when they hit the skin. Soon they poured down with a vengeance soaking all the animals in the field.

It rained so hard Stinky could barely see ten feet in front of him. The water started running across the pasture in small rivulets quickly swelling into larger streams.

Low areas of the pasture began filling up with water. Almost before the cows knew fully what was happening, the water had risen almost to their knees. They began bawling loudly over and over, their sounds high-pitched and scary to hear. Around the pasture they splashed, frantically searching along the fence for a way out. All felt trapped and terrified.

As the rains poured down, the water rose, soon reaching almost to the top of their legs. The cows continued bawling in panic, the whites of their eyes wide with fear. "The Five Rules of the Herd" seemed to have flown away with the wind and out of everyone's minds. Adding to the water, chaos filled their little cow world completely.

The only good news that remained were the calves, now almost full grown, had enough height like their mothers to buy them a little more time for a solution before the rising water had its way. Being shorter than the cows, Stinky had considerably less time before he'd be forced to start swimming.

With time literally running out, Stinky blinked the excess water out of his eyes one more time. They cleared well enough for him to spy a large, round hay bale setting at the top of the hill near the barn. In that split second, hope flickered. He began moving to the hay bale fast as he possibly could, partly jumping through the beating rain, slippery mud and ever-deepening waters on the ground.

His quick thinking and reactions paid off as he reached the hay bale. Almost immediately, he reared back on his two hind legs and jumped as high as he could

STINKY DISCOVERS AN ESCAPE

landing solidly with all four feet on top of the wet hay bale. From atop he could see one of the pasture gates in the fence not too far away.

Four questions zoomed through his head all at once at lightning speed, *"Could I reach the gate from here if I tried to jump over to it?* Then he spied a wire latch holding the gate closed and thought out loud, *"Could I grab that wire loop in my mouth in the few seconds I'd have when I jumped? And after hopefully landing, could I actually pull the gate wide open for the cows to escape the pasture? Could I really move them out to higher ground?"*

Stinky sensed he didn't have time to ponder his chances any longer. He needed to act right then. He began baa-baa-baaing loud as he could over and over, finally catching Clara's attention. She began her alarm bawling louder than any cow cries heard before in the field. The two of them created enough noise to gain the attention of the rest of the herd. Clara and the herd waded through the water as fast as they could over to the hay bale with Stinky still standing on top like king of the mountain.

In the meantime, Stinky gathered all his strength and thrust himself off the bale of hay, leaping through the air and beating rain like some kind of flying, white, wet, wild thing. His landing onto the gate wasn't pretty, more like straddling it with his legs, but he made it okay. Even more importantly, he landed close enough to the wire loop and grabbed it in his mouth using his teeth to work the latch up and over the post.

To his amazement, the gate popped open and easily swung wide and clear! He didn't waste another second. He jumped off the now open gate, actually more like fell off it, and then helped Clara lead the cows to higher ground and safety. Huddled and greatly relieved, the cows and Stinky waited out the rest of the storm together.

After the storm passed, everything changed in the cowherd. Stinky transitioned into hero status, revered for his cleverness and courage. Perhaps even more interesting was once he became such a hero and all, the cows not only tolerated his peculiar issues, they no longer could see, hear, or smell them. Approval and love moved in to Stinky's heart and sadness moved out for good. Stinky had finally arrived home, truly home at last, and all felt right in the world.

On any day, at any given time you might be able to catch the sound of the animals cheering Stinky as he walks by them. Their cheers still sound more like a rap, but the verse goes something like this:

"Here comes that Stinky Putz,
Our hero, no matter what's;
So stand, salute, when he walks by
Cuz this jumping goat is quite a guy!"

Juicy Animal Facts From Tale Six: Stinky, the Goat Who Would Be Cow

Blazed-faced cow—is a red colored cow with a distinct white blaze on its face. Cows with such color markings are called Herefords.

Walking-in-line-and-in-order—represents a type of social order commonly seen in many mammals (elephants, gorillas, wolves, etc.) and birds that live in groups. The order of walking, eating, drinking, etc., is determined by factors such as age, size, and intelligence. Their position in the order determines when they can eat as well as their position in the walking lineup.

White, puffy wind clouds—are generally called *cumulous* clouds and look like white cotton. *Cumulonimbus* clouds look like white puffs in dark gray or blue and can bring heavy rain, snow, sleet and other strong weather.

TALE SEVEN

THE CHAMELEON'S NEW SMILE

Before actually getting into the meat of this next story, Ezra began sharing some background about the chameleon with Sally Scott to whet her appetite a bit. What he didn't know about the girl riding on his back was how chameleons ranked as one of her most favorite animals. Funny how that works sometimes.

He was not just any lizard. Not by a long shot. He was a chameleon, and a most charming one at that. Even his name was, well, distinctive for a lizard. His name was Niles, and Niles could charm the socks off most any unpleasant critter to venture his way. For a little lizard in a great big jungle, charm like his was a gift. But I'm getting a little ahead of myself.

Niles lived back in ancient times in an enormous jungle where trees grew so close to each other it forced sunlight to slip through determinedly in long slender threads. Most days Niles hung out up in the treetops along with his buddy chameleons and looked for food—much safer up there than on the ground.

Niles possessed an awesomely long tail he used like an extra, really long finger to wrap around tree branches and keep him from falling. He ate just about anything including snails and worms but admitted they were pretty gross choices. He much preferred some nice crunchy ants or something close, but he certainly wouldn't pass up on some juicy fruits or flowers should he happen upon them. All in all, I guess Niles might be described best as an *opportunist* when it came to food.

Also common in all chameleons, Niles' body had two exceptional tools to help him get food, the absolute most important job he faced each and every day. First were his eyes. While he couldn't hear worth beans, he had very good eyesight for a reptile. From fifteen feet away he could spot a colorless cicada clutching a tree trunk for dear life and, if that wasn't enough, Niles could look in two directions at the same time!

Equally impressive, his second tool featured an extraordinary rocket-like tongue. Just like his super long tail, his chameleon tongue extended unusually long as reptile tongues go. Niles could whip his out at lightning speed to more than twice the length of his body! Any unfortunate bug zapped by Niles' tongue never knew what hit him it happened so fast.

Niles' body supplied him with yet another thing particularly helpful when he searched for food. At the tip of his incredibly long, incredibly fast, and incredibly sticky tongue, a bunch of little suction cup gripper type thingies allowed him to grip his prey and hold it fast and tight. Like I said, Niles had an awesome tongue.

But when Niles had to deal with conflicts, even his body's great food-getting tools simply weren't enough. You see, being a chameleon put him closer to the bottom of the jungle food chain where he could more easily become the prey of larger animals. That unfortunate fact tended to make conflicts a lot more challenging for Niles and his friends. For example, Niles negotiated with a hunger-crazed bunch of screaming monkeys one time to keep them from eating him right there on the spot. On another day he talked a large hawk into changing his dinner plans so he wasn't on the menu, so to speak. Niles' conflicts also involved convincing new female chameleons how he was definitely the best pick of boyfriends for them, but that's another story altogether.

The scariness of conflict seemed far less troubling to Niles than the irritation it caused him, like a conspiracy of interruptions to his food finding. And because conflict sometimes came in different forms, it prevented Niles from planning in advance for how to deal with it. Nooooo–that would be too easy. Conflict had an annoying way of keeping you guessing.

Sometimes conflict would sneak up on Niles. He saw these as *"silent but deadlies."* Always the worst of conflict situations, they often involved a snake of some sort. Snakes could climb up to the top of the trees where the chameleons hung out, and those slithering snake guys kept so quiet you never heard them coming. Unfortunately, snakes really liked the taste of chameleon.

The good news for Niles came early on in his life when he realized he had a gift for making him quite good at dealing with conflict in its many different forms. *"Superb"* describes more aptly his talent in this area. And he worked hard at improving those skills, too. Eventually in almost any form conflict took, Niles could handle it. He became a master at using his wit and charm to disarm whatever animal tried to eat him or give him a hard time. He'd always manage to turn the situation around with his brilliant smile, flattering words, and good humor.

Then one day most unexpectedly, everything changed. After stuffing himself all morning with literally a dozen fat, crunchy insects and feeling quite pleasant, Niles decided to take a little snooze. A brilliant idea came to him. He'd try napping on the ground for a change. At least it seemed brilliant in that moment anyway.

He took his time slowly climbing down from his high tree limb as less light shone with the late afternoon sun drooping down in the sky. He stretched out on the ground near a rainbow of lovely, blooming flowers, their aroma entirely intoxicating. He thought he'd scrounge around later for what other tasty treats might lay hidden in the loose leaves there.

As evening approached, Niles snored away dreaming with a big smile on his face about all those secret things only chameleons dream about. Unfortunately, his sweet, happy mind wanderings began to crumble when a rumbling thunderstorm, or so he thought, arrived unannounced into his dream world. His eyes opened just a bit to form a tiny slit for him to check out this latest uninvited interruption.

In a nano-second Niles sprang to attention, fully awakened by the sight of a giant, close-up face of a most unpleasant looking fox staring back at him through hungry eyes. Niles' mouth dropped wide open in total surprise and then he froze. He remained way too scared to close his mouth or his eyes.

Like most foxes, the one facing him had the reputation as a *"trickster."* Animal tricksters slyly tricked other animals into doing stupid stuff at their own expense—like those in Native American stories where coyotes tricked turkeys to become their food or otters once tricked bears to lose their tails, and so on.

Niles worried, thinking to himself, *"How does one trickster outwit another trickster? Hmmm."* He decided to remain quiet and completely motionless when he heard the fox beginning to growl through his already contorted looking face. Conjuring up a big dose of charm simply did not seem like a good option for Niles at the moment.

The fox's upper lip started to snarl, curling up to

reveal some nasty looking pointed teeth. His eyes grew much darker now and his look pierced Niles like two daggers. Niles sensed if he moved even the slightest smidgeon, it would trigger the fox's mouth like a *Venus Fly Trap* snapping shut on a moth, and he'd be a goner in seconds. Wisely, he continued on with his excellent rock impersonation.

But the fox's patience wore thin. He'd begun his day trying to outwit a couple of rabbits, but wound up getting mud stuck way up his nostrils when he attempted to pull them out of their tunnel. Following that unpleasant fiasco, the fox had engaged in a brief, spirited confrontation with a family of brazen raccoons. Obvious prisoners of their own scarcity mentality, the raccoons remained stubbornly unwilling to share even the smallest morsel of several nice sized fish they'd scored earlier. A run-in with a grumpy snapping turtle followed a staring contest with a great horned owl. All these unpleasantries had worked together to sour his mood for the now troubling situation before him with the little chameleon.

The fox's stomach began rumbling quietly. He'd become so focused on the chameleon he hadn't realized how hungry he'd become. He feared the chameleon would dart off if he moved to eat him, but he needed to end the current stalemate. During their staring contest, he tried to think how he might tempt the chameleon to let down his guard.

Like a statue in freeze tag Niles held true, but he began to tire a bit holding his body position without any movement at all. He could hardly believe his eyes when he spied an absolutely enormous great blue heron come flying out of nowhere with his spear-like beak pointed right at him. He thought to himself, *"Really? What is it with this day?"*

The heron looked like he'd fallen straight from outer space with only one thing on his mind—stabbing Niles for dinner. A second later, the fox, too, caught movement out of the corner of his eye and looked up at the incoming heron for a moment to shoo it away. In that split second Niles managed to steal several inches away, safely sliding back in front of the flowers growing nearby. The fox showed more of his teeth, intimidating the heron enough to make it reconsider and zoom off seeking some other poor victim.

But when the fox turned his attention back to the chameleon, Niles was nowhere in sight. The fox sensed the chameleon's close presence and he could smell him well enough but he couldn't see him. After the miserable day he'd already had, the fox's frustration reached its limits. It made him want that measly chameleon all the more.

Niles could clearly see the fox before him losing patience. It scared him horribly but at the same time he wondered why the fox couldn't see him right there in front of him. Then he remembered feeling the strange warming sensation at the tip of his tail when he'd first opened his eyes from his nap to see a giant fox face a breath away.

In the whirl of everything happening, Niles had

forgotten how the strange sensation seemed to move up his tail like a slow lava flow and then across his back and down into his legs, over his chest and finally over the top of his head and face. He remembered how it didn't hurt. It actually had felt fairly comforting like the way a smile spreads. He hadn't resisted it, just went with it in the moment. Recalling the strange feeling again didn't make Niles feel any less puzzled at the moment. Somehow, he continued to resist moving any part of his body.

Finally, after unsuccessfully searching intensely for the chameleon, frustration had its way with the fox. He snorted once loudly and trotted off, abandoning his mission.

Niles felt greatly relieved but still very puzzled and asked himself over and over, *"Why would the fox leave when I was right there in front of him?"* He could find no answer, no clue, not even a hint. He smartly decided to climb back up into the safety of the tall trees and wasted no time doing so. Once back with the other chameleons, one chameleon after another asked him similar questions about his appearance:

"What has happened to your body? How'd you get all those colors? Can you feel the colors? How do you make them change like that?

It took a while but together the chameleons figured it out. Apparently, Niles had become so frightened by his encounter with the fox and the heron that his body made color changes in his skin. The colors had cloaked him,

FOX LOSES SIGHT OF NILES

making his body almost invisible against the colorful flowers behind him.

What happened to Niles marked the first time a chameleon had experienced all over color changes in the body. Not long after Niles' "colorful" event, such changes became a typical response for many types of chameleons all over the world.

Niles realized he no longer needed to depend entirely on his charm, wit, and big smiles alone to protect him and get out of tough situations. He had a different kind of smile now—one that begins in his tail and spreads like a rainbow of color across him.

Juicy Animal Facts From Tale Seven:
The Chameleon's New Smile

Opportunist—means he eats whatever comes along first, either plants or animals or both. The scientific term for the chameleon's eating habits is *omnivore*, in other words, he eats both plants and animals.

Food chain—refers to the position or order of animals according to who eats whom.

Trickster—is the term in Native American, African and other folklore that describes animal characters who typically outsmart or trick other animals in order to take advantage and benefit.

Venus Flytrap—is a type of plant that attracts, then snaps shut to trap mainly insects and spiders, digesting them to provide needed nutrients lacking in the sandy soil where they grow in eastern North Carolina and South Carolina.

Animal skin color changes—in chameleons are not yet totally understood. They are chemically caused and related to emotional changes the animal is feeling. Somewhat like when a human blushes, but more complex. Other animals that change their color include the Dwarf Cuttlefish, Peacock Flounder, Squid, Octopus, and the White Crab Spider among others.

Scarcity Mentality—is more than selfishness; it's an underlying *"not enough to go around"* attitude some humans have that shows itself in many different ways.

WHITE FEATHERS

About to begin his eighth tale, Ezra, the old storyteller, first let his friend Sally Scott know how much he just loved this next story. "It may have happened long ago but its message to us is timeless," he told her.

Besides the magpies, all the big blackbirds including cousins like the crows and the ravens, called her "queen of the magpies" or just "Queenie" for short, and not out of any respect either. Ever since she'd been a wee bird growing up in the American West, she'd acted like she was better than all the other magpies, like they were beneath her or something.

Queenie clearly owned vanity as her most out-standing personal trait. While sun bathing she held her head down and her back facing the sun, showing off by scratching with one foot reaching up and clear over the top of her bird head to get the itch on the other side. She snuck moments to catch a glimpse of her own reflection in any water she might happen upon. She'd stand there turning this way and that, thoroughly admiring her body from different viewpoints.

Most of all Queenie loved looking at her covering of shiny all black feathers as well as her exceptionally long, pointed tail highlighted in brilliant, iridescent blue-green colors, and her simply fabulous long black beak. After such ego-gazing, she'd walk around doing the typical magpie *strut,* swaggering about kind of cocky-like trying to capture everyone's attention so they could admire her too.

One year, along with hundreds of other magpies, Queenie attended a very large assembly of her kind. Called a "Parliament," these gatherings reportedly had been so named from the large groups congregating together in early spring, looking very stately while cawing at each other and causing quite a ruckus. If the truth be known, most birds had come to simply flirt and share gossip.

During Queenie's first Parliament and without any effort whatsoever on Queenie's part, her beauty captured the attention and ultimate devotion of a young male magpie attending the event purposely to find a mate. Afterwards, he returned with her and the rest of her small group back to their colony. He and Queenie soon began to plan a nest-building venture together.

Unfortunately, building a nest together became a nightmare for the new couple. They couldn't even decide on where it should be built. They argued and argued and eventually built separate nests. Actually, it was more like the poor male went out and collected all the sticks and twigs and such and did all the hard labor. For almost two months he built two gigantic, distinctively magpie-domed nests high in the treetops in two different trees no less.

Queenie happily took on the interior decorating aspects for the new nests. She covered the interior with soft mosses and grasses over a mud-cemented bottom. She couldn't resist adding a few small, shiny, flat stones she'd picked up along the river's edge so she could have the effect of mirrors all about to admire herself when she'd soon be sitting in the nest on the eggs for such long stretches of time.

Many seemed surprised when Queenie rose to the occasion of motherhood and impressed everyone with her devotion to duty. In spite of her usual selfishness, she actually became an excellent mother. After her babies fledged the nest and became members of their colony, Queenie had an interesting revelation—her mate was a *"Yes mam"* kind of bird who relied on her and wouldn't or couldn't think for himself. It only served to further convince Queenie of her superiority over everyone else.

As time passed, Queenie successfully worked her way up to the top of the magpie social ladder. She first ascended within her own intimate colony of eight family members. Next, she rose to the top of the *"pecking order"* in larger assemblies when a number of small groups combined for a particular event. As the alpha bird, she essentially served as the leader of her small group of magpies and often when larger groups of them met as well. Maybe she got to the top because she was so bossy. She was good at that.

Admittedly, it must be a difficult job for any bird attempting to manage a bunch of magpies, a lot like herding butterflies in many ways. Magpies are just too smart for their own feathers. Widely known among all the animals is how magpies rank among the top five smartest animals in the animal kingdom. They're right up there with humans, chimpanzees, dolphins, and elephants!

Unfortunately, Queenie's obnoxious selfishness greatly compromised her smarts. It may explain why she lacked all the important qualities for making her a good leader over the long term. Smarts and bravery without compassion is only foolishness—foolish trickery of one's self. Queenie nagged others rather than giving clear directives so everyone understood. She pecked on them, too, rather than inspiring them to take some action. In general, she focused on mastering the art of self-indulgence rather than on hard work and caring for her group.

Shamelessly, Queenie even stole food from her subordinates at times. Routinely she collected ticks off the backs of whatever large mammal she found to safely perch upon. Sometimes a mule deer, sometimes a moose, or occasionally she sat on a tired, old, bull buffalo.

After she ate a few of the ticks, she'd collect a bunch of others in her mouth then fly off somewhere, peck a little hole in the ground and carefully drop the ticks in it. She'd cover her secret storage with loose leaves, saving the ticks for a tasty snack later on. Before flying off, she'd cock her head to one side so she could get a good look at exactly the spot where she'd hidden them away in her *cache*. But sometimes she'd just spy on others to see where they were hiding their ticks, then she'd go steal them for easy pickings.

Perhaps because Queenie acted so full of herself it may explain why she so often engaged in *self-anointing* behaviors. The bottom line was if it made her feel good, she was all about it. *"Besides, I am the Queen and I deserve such indulgence,"* she'd say to herself, then she'd go find a large number of ants on an anthill or crawling around on something rotting. She'd carefully pick them up one by one with her beak and place them on her feathers. After putting a bunch of them on herself, she'd sit back and enjoy the effect of the cleansing chemicals they released on her skin beneath her feathers. She always felt more refreshed after such rituals.

For kicks, Queenie loved wreaking terror on innocent prairie dogs. She looked down on them as stupid and deserving whatever came to them. From their tunnels underground they could hear her growly voice as she flew down to their community from above. *"Chat, chat, chat"* she taunted along with some occasional hissing under her breath just to tease and torment them.

Queenie patiently waited in absolute silence for one of their little heads to pop up out of a hole so she could swoop down, bang her wings up and down and scare them out of their wits. Queenie thought of prairie dogs as mostly too large and chubby to make a habit out of hunting them. Harassing them offered a good second best.

Queenie forced her intimate group of magpies to remain on the lookout for prairie dog settlements, or *dog towns*. The closest dog town to her magpie colony existed a short flight away. It occupied an open grassy area with only a couple of trees on the edge. About two hundred dirt mounds made up this underground prairie dog community of tunnels with front and rear entrances.

One day while stalking the dog town, Queenie hid behind a nearby clump of sagebrush and waited patiently for a furry head to pop up,. Unbeknownst to Queenie, a large red-tailed hawk flew high above also scoping out the dog town. He spotted her poking her head in and out from behind the sagebrush every now and then. That tiny bit of movement gave the hawk's keen eyes all they needed to get a fix on her. He regularly feasted on the prairie dogs but an unsuspecting magpie might add a nice side dish to his dinner.

Besides hawks, the prairie dogs had to watch out for many other types of predators as well, including eagles, foxes, coyotes, black-footed ferrets, and bobcats. Not an easy thing for the prairie dogs who had to constantly find the courage to perch atop their mounds so they could spy danger outside and signal the others to take cover.

Of all the predators who hunted and killed them for food they feared the hawks and eagles the most. The *raptors* flew so far up in the sky and attacked with such amazing speed, the prairie dogs often never saw the danger coming until too late.

Unable to wait any longer, Queenie flew excitedly over to a mound and began chattering, growling and making her best, obnoxious, scary noises down into the hole. Hearing no response, she poked her head into the entrance hole and snapped her beak open and shut for an even more terrifying affect. She could hear the scared prairie dogs scampering around down in the tunnel. She imagined them all huddled together shivering in absolute fear just a little farther inside.

With her patience wearing thin, she began thinking how fun it might be to continue her chase of them a bit more up close and personal. She ducked her head and half wiggled, half hopped through the opening and down into the tunnel a bit further. It was a tight fit. She heard a couple of prairie dogs barking behind her above ground but chose to ignore them.

That's when the unimaginable struck like lightning and without warning. Throughout the tunnels the sounds of hundreds of terrified prairie dogs rang out at the same time. They barked and screamed loudly. A brief pause followed, perhaps the silence even more terrifying.

Then a giant, clawed, scaly hawk's leg stretched out slowly moving down the dark tunnel. Each of its sharp, long talons reached out, feeling along as it went. The red-tailed hawk hoped he'd get lucky and snag a prairie dog or the magpie, either would work just fine.

Since Queenie's body faced down the tunnel, her back faced the hawk. She couldn't see exactly what was happening behind her but she could hear the prairie dogs continuing to sound their frenzied alarms. She knew something bad was happening. Then, just as two giant talons began to close in around the sides of her body, several prairie dogs grabbed her and pulled and tugged, coaxing her all the while to move further down the tunnel to safety.

They couldn't speak magpie to her but somehow she knew they meant her no harm. Her body slipped away from the hawk's grasp, but its deadly talons managed to scrape against her shoulders on both sides of her body ripping out some of her outside feathers completely.

The sound of Queenie's screams from the pain reached the magpies waiting for her not too far away. They flew straight to the hawk with its one leg still down the prairie dog hole. The sight of seven magpies zooming in on him while he struggled in such an awkward position required an immediate response on his part. Somehow the hawk pulled himself together and flew away.

The magpies stayed with Queenie until the prairie dogs helped her to back out of the tunnel. And the magpies helped her get back to their colony of nests. They attended her needs with great kindness until she finally recuperated fully. Then they all put their heads together to come up with a plan to work together to drive the hawk away for good.

During this time, Queenie changed. She realized the brave thing the prairie dogs had done to save her and promised to never harass or bully prairie dogs, or anything else again. And she realized how her magpie family had stayed by her side. She finally understood the importance of compassion and caring about others. She promised herself she'd always make it part of her whole being from then on. Her greatest revelation came when she realized the blame for her near demise had been entirely hers alone.

Queenie resumed her role as alpha leader with renewed zeal. To help plan a mob attack to drive the hawk away, she brought in several other magpie family groups from the surrounding area. Together they drove the hawk far away for good. News of their success travelled fast and far. So great was their team feat, it became legendary among the magpies.

New plumage eventually sprouted from the injured areas where Queenie had lost feathers to the hawk. Strangely, her new feathers grew back not black but white as snow. Eventually, with each *molt* of her feathers, most of the feathers on her wings were replaced with partially white ones.

Even more amazing, every magpie born after Queenie's narrow escape had the same white patches of feathers in the same areas as Queenie's. Some say the distinct white plumage in all magpies today stands as a reminder of Queenie's hard lessons in humility and the importance of compassion in order to have happiness and lasting success as a leader.

After he'd finished telling the story about Queenie, Ezra added, *"To this day, the high value of compassion magpies show can be seen in the funerals they take part in when a loved one dies. They pick flowers with their beaks and place the flowers, like bouquets, on the site of the departed bird. The magpies will sit unusually quiet with no chatter for fifteen minutes or so, and then suddenly depart."*

QUEENIE (CENTER AT BOTTOM) AND FRIENDS
LEAVE FLOWERS AT MAGPIE FUNERAL

Juicy Animal Facts From *Tale* *Eight: White Feathers*

Strut—is a common, distinctive walking gait of magpies featuring a swagger, moving their bodies one way and then another way.

Parliament—is the term for large groups of magpies together so named after the governing body in Great Britain who demonstrate some similar behaviors in common.

Cache—is a hiding place for storing stuff until needed later. Magpies commonly create a cache to hide their goodies.

Self-anointing behavior—in magpies, is the practice of putting ants on their bodies. There is no agreement as to the purpose. Possibly it's to kill mites, bacteria or fungus on their bodies or to cleanse the preen oil on their feathers. Other mammals such as hedgehogs and some dogs,

for example, also anoint themselves with certain smelly things only they can appreciate and enjoy.

Raptors—is the biological term for hawks and eagles that also prey on other birds.

Talons—are the impressive long, sharp claws at the end of each hawk or other raptors' toes.

Molt—refers to birds' periodic shedding of old feathers in various places on their body and the beginning growth of new replacement feathers. All the birds' feathers do not molt at the same time so a bird can always fly.

TALE NINE

THE BLUE LIGHT MYSTERY

As he prepared to tell this next story, Ezra first settled into some cool green grass and made himself comfortable. Next, he took care to impress upon his friend and scribe, Sally Scott, this story's importance for all children everywhere. He told her he believed it was one of those wonders of nature no one could explain then or now, especially how the animals could talk and understand each other as well as human words. Who knows, it may well have been a miracle.

It was a strange time. Something felt different. You could almost smell it in the air. At least that's the way it felt for many animals outside in the wild places. They whispered, hissed and chattered nervously among each other, *"What's happening? Something doesn't feel right."*

More and more animals began acting out their growing sense of uneasiness, and often in bizarre ways. Instead of focusing as usual on living their terribly busy lives doing this or that, many of the same kinds of animals got the jitters so bad they began to switch from just worrying about their uneasiness to chattering amongst themselves in small groups. They figured maybe somebody else knew something they didn't.

Squirrels stopped looking for nuts and sat around in groups trying in vain to figure out what's up. Groups of birds began flying around in circles hoping to see what might be causing their unrest. Wolves and coyotes howled for no reason other than sounding out an alarm. Deer grouped together with their fawns and tried to come up with some explanation that made sense. And on it went to no avail. They all sensed they'd lost something, something important. *"But what they wondered?"*

Perhaps their biggest discovery was finding everyone as confused and worried as they were. It didn't take long before all the different animals reached the same conclusion—they faced a mystery of a very high order of importance and they simply weren't going to be able to figure it out all by themselves. From the cloud of mysterious uneasiness, fear rose among the animals and quickly moved among them like a mighty forest fire.

Various kinds of older, senior animals remembered hearing stories from the past about a time long ago when animals had benefitted by working together, achieving something otherwise unimaginable. Those animals of another era also had faced an enormous problem. They gave credit for solving it to having held what was called a *Great Meeting.*

Apparently, since ancient times, a Great Meeting had been a rare animal assembly that dealt with only the very, very, most important of issues. Most of these senior animals agreed the last Great Meeting had to do with lots of ice and things getting very cold, or something like that. And that particular Great Meeting took place long ago, before the births of any of those senior animals, or their parents, or their parents' parents—more likely thousands of generations before any of them had been born.

News traveled fast in the animal world. Soon many agreed that having their own Great Meeting might be the best way to come together peacefully and listen to each other. They hoped maybe one of them had already figured out the cause of the creepy weirdness everyone sensed. Maybe a solution lay just ahead.

A time and place for their Great Meeting was set, and a good many animals took comfort by this decision. While only a small step of an action, it certainly felt a lot better than just sitting around bumping their gums worrying.

For their upcoming big event, representatives of the animals from all over began traveling, some for considerable distances to get there. But get there they did: big animals and small ones, fast animals and veeerrry slooooow ones, fancy ones and interesting ones, fierce brave ones and timid shy ones too–far too many to name here for sure.

Over time wild animals of many kinds arrived for their Great Meeting at a place where big loose rocks from nearby high places had spilled-down on an inlet near the ocean's edge. Tall stately trees offered their leafy canopies for shade. It was quiet and protected there. The predawn light had an unusual soft purplish glow to it, and the air smelled salty and nice there too. The peaceful specialness of the place created a perfect setting for their odd assembly.

After everyone arrived, the animals nervously agreed they needed one more important thing to make their Great Meeting a success. They needed super good leadership to uphold a truce. On everyone's mind was the plain fact that some animals were the natural hunters of other animals. This stark reality complicated matters for working well together.

For the first time in a very, very long while, differences needed to be temporarily set aside so all the animals could put their minds totally on the important business at hand. Why? Because they all felt the problem at hand was much bigger than any one individual's needs or wants. They didn't yet *know* this as fact, but they strongly sensed it. So strongly that for them it felt the same as knowing with certainty.

After remarkably little argument the animals agreed in short order to ask two particularly trustworthy individuals to lead them at this time: a highly respected bald eagle and a well-known great horned owl.

"BAYLEK"

"STELLA"

The owl and the eagle made a most unusual leadership duo, both being predators, but all the animals felt they faced a most unusual situation and this pair of leaders made for the perfect sleuths to help them with it. This particular owl and this particular eagle excelled at being steady in the midst of confusion swirling around them. Unlike many other animals that by their nature could easily be distracted, these leaders had what it took to stay on purpose.

Widely revered, Stella, the great horned owl, stood out for several reasons. For starters, she had wisdom beyond measure and she was a most excellent listener. She also possessed truly amazing eyesight, superbly, uniquely effective even at night.

Like all owls, Stella also had specially shaped wing feathers allowing the wind to pass over them in perfect silence. She could fly very fast even in the darkest and thickest of woods without creating any sound at all and without head crashing into anything either. Not even a *whewwww* or a *swooosh*! Rightfully so, everyone knew the great horned owl as the silent, stealth commander of the night!

Baylek, the bald eagle chosen by the animals, did not like being called a *bald* eagle. After all, he wasn't bald, and he really didn't like being called something he was not. His imposing head-covering of white feathers actually created a rather royal appearance for him—a crown almost. And Baylek's giant wings could spread over seven feet when he unfurled them all the way. He had great strength and the sharpest of eyes. Rumors reported he could spot a flopping fish at a river's edge from a mile away.

Another of Baylek's admirable traits may have been a lot less flashy but way more important. When he gave his word on something, all the animals knew with confidence they could count on him. Like the time when he and his mate had three eggs in their nest and Baylek's turn came to sit over them and keep them warm so they could hatch. But a fierce, early spring snowstorm blew in unexpectedly and gradually covered the nest completely with its freezing cold load of snow.

It also buried Baylek until only the very tip of his beak poking through a tiny hole in the snow remained visible. But he never left those eggs, not once, even though it snowed all day and all night. Baylek took his responsibilities very seriously.

The Great Meeting finally began just as hints of first light sneaked in through the trees. Gradually, the sun rose like a fireball in the sky illuminating all the animals gathered on the beach. They excitedly scurried about, arranging themselves in a wide circle at the waters edge so everyone present could see everyone else. A few animals, like a sea turtle, a pair of otters, and a school of dolphin, lived in the ocean's waters and just swam right up close to shore to attend the meeting.

From somewhere a gentle breeze lightly ruffled Baylek and Stella's feathers as they sat perched on a large, silvery piece of sea-worn driftwood gracefully jutting out from the sand. The two appeared rather regal sitting there together as Stella spoke first: *"Today is an important time for us. We've come together to solve a mystery, to find out what this thing is we're all feeling. From where is it coming? Why do we all sense it so strongly? What may it mean?"*

Everyone nodded, so Stella kept going: *"Today we shall listen to everyone who has come here and to all you have to share about the situation. With ears of compassion we must listen to each other to hear about what you've seen from where you've come. And tonight you can continue to discuss together your observations while I fly through the forests and trees, meadows and hills, parks and cities. I'll listen to the whispers of the wind in the willows. I'll look for any hints to this mystery that may lay hidden below me.*

Stella looked over at Baylek and he picked up where she'd left off, saying, *"Early tomorrow morning I will soar high above us, higher than the mountaintops. I'll look down from afar. Together Stella and I will find what clues are out there."*

"After we've both returned we must all be ready to hear the truth and consider what we must do next," Baylek and Stella said together with utmost sincerity in their voices.

When Stella addressed the group of animals, she slowly moved her head around as only owls can. It looked odd, like her head was going all the way around in a complete circle. It struck a few of the animals funny, but no one dared laugh, especially with her owl-stare piercing right into the eyes of each of them as she spoke. It felt a little creepy, as if she was looking right through them, but it served to hold their attention quite well.

SALLY SCOTT GUYNN

STELLA FLIES NIGHT RECONNAISSANCE

Each animal took turns, one by one, giving their ideas and sharing their feelings before the group. No one interrupted. It became an important part of their peace agreement with each other. As such, during the Great Meeting there'd be no chasing, biting, growling, teasing, snarling, hissing, snapping or any other not-so-nice behavior, including interrupting.

The day of listening came and went with no apparent solutions. Night followed and Stella completed her mission as planned, hearing and seeing all she could.

On the next day with the sun's first light on his back, Baylek flew far and wide covering great distances, seeing what he also could observe.

That same afternoon when Baylek returned to the Great Meeting, he found the nervous animals waiting together but barely able to hold still any longer with their curiosity and jitters cresting over the top. Tails wagged back and forth, flippers slapped together loudly, and tongues darted in and out. Fur bristled. Feathers puffed. None could remember a time with so much excitement.

Baylek flapped his enormous wings a couple of times, signaling he was ready to speak. Instantly, everyone became as still and quiet as the summer air before a storm: *"You all have spoken,"* he began. *"You have also listened well. Stella and I have flown our missions and scouted the lands and waters."* Baylek seemed to be having some trouble getting the right words out next. *"We agree we all seem to share a feeling of ... a feeling of ... loss. We are sensing great loss. We ... may have ... lost something that means ... that means everything to us. Something bigger and more important than ourselves."*

A shudder suddenly crept through the gathering of animals. As one, they sensed they were about to hear something even more troubling. Baylek continued, speaking very deliberately, *"From flying and looking down from way above, the greatest thing that appears to be missing is ... well, you're just not going to believe me when I tell you ..."* His voice then trailed off 'til none could hear him.

All the animals jumped up at the same time and shouted, *"Whaaat? Tell us!"*

Baylek took a deep breath and tried again: *"Very well. Here it is. The thing definitely missing from us, from nature, is* **children***—the children of humans."*

A gut-sucking gasp escaped from the crowd of listeners pressed in now more closely together so they wouldn't miss a word. Eyes widened. Mouths hung in dumbfounded amazement at what they were hearing.

"Children? Human children? Missing? Huh?" they cried.

Trying to be clearer still, Baylek added: *"Let me explain. We have no reports of children playing or spending any time outdoors with nature. No bird feeding, no bike riding, no building forts, no berry picking. Nothing. Nada."*

For several minutes the group of animals sat on the beach very still and very, very quiet. They had heard Baylek's words, but the words didn't make complete sense. *"How can children, human children, be missing?"*

they wondered. *"They are, after all, **human**. And humans are #1, numero uno, top of the food chain, totally in control, smart. Real smart!"*

Stella cleared her throat, ruffling up some feathers around her neck area making her look slightly more majestic. She began addressing the crowd of animals again, but more slowly in a serious, clear voice: *"I must agree with Baylek. As I flew the night, I saw no giggling children outside catching lightning bugs, no little boys digging up earthworms to go fishing the next morning with grandpa, and no girls and boys swinging, playing tag, or making shadow figures with their flashlights.*

But I did see something that might be important -- a strange blue light glowed from the windows of all the human houses. It's where most of the children seemed to be gathered ... inside, near the glow of the blue lights. Very curious. Made me wonder about it indeed."

"Stop, please stop!" cried Twiloby, a bright-eyed chipmunk who lived in a woodpile with her family of five babies, or her *'Twilly Chips'* as everyone called them for short. *"That's quite enough information for the moment. The poor kids! Oh, what **are** we to do? We must do **something**! But we're **only** animals for heaven's sake!"* she cried nervously, puffing her cheeks in and out, in and out, in short bursts.

Stella answered, her voice steady and direct with her usual owlish ability to focus right in, laser-like, on the most important thing at the moment: *"Okay, listen up! The human children are not missing from **everywhere**;*

*they are missing from the **out-of-doors**! Read-my-beak friends: the human children are no longer going **outside to play**."*

Bingo. There it was—mystery revealed, at least in part. All the animals sitting around the circle realized they had just heard a great truth.

Stella continued: *"This explains what we've all been sensing: the silence in the woods ... the lonely calmness on the lakes ... the lack of joy in the air. It all makes sense now, doesn't it? The absence of the sounds of human children waking up a park with their laughter, or stirring up a creek's waters with their kicking feet ... hearing them chasing butterflies while running through the grass, or digging holes, tracking ants, and climbing trees. Without these things, without **them**, the balance in nature goes out of whack. And we **all** lose ... nature loses and children lose too. And not just for now but for **our children** and their children!"*

Slowly, the undeniable truth crept in. One by one, the animals raised their heads and nodded, asking *"But why? Human children used to love to play outdoors!"*

Then everyone began chattering, squeaking and squawking all at once.

Finally Baylek spread his spectacular wings all the way out, arched his neck and spoke calmly in a most kingly voice to his once again instantly hushed audience. *"Remember this: Often the scariest things are when you must face something and you don't know clearly what it is or why.* Baylek paused a moment to give his listeners time to let the profound words sink in all the way.

His audience remained very quiet and still. Baylek picked up where he'd left off, speaking in a low, clear and serious voice: *"This problem we now share is of the highest order. Somehow we all know this. We can lick our paws, stretch our claws, or howl at the moon 'til we turn purple, but it still won't change anything. It won't bring the children back to nature, back to the outdoors. For **that**, we'll need a plan! We'll need to work **together** and we'll need to work **fast**. Madame Owl, please share your ideas with us now."*

Stella picked up where Baylek left off without hesitation. *"First, we must let all the animals know about this problem. Get the crows in the East and their cousins, the ravens and magpies in the West. They're smart and they'll quickly figure out how to noisily spread the word to the rest of the animals on the ground. And, oh yes, get the seagulls to spread the word to the animals in the oceans and the bays."*

"But how can all the animals help? What's the rest of our plan?" asked a little sparrow jumping up and down in excitement while perched on the antlers of a very large bull moose and trying her best not to lose her grip.

Stella replied: *"Our plan of action has two parts really. First, we must let **all** the animals know we've lost the children from nature and the balance is out of whack. Second, each one of us plus all the animals we reach can work in different ways to get the message to the young humans to come back outside and play. Bottomline, that is our key message we must get out to the humans!"*

Baylek added one more important piece for the animals to consider when he said, *"Stella and I believe the problem is so important we may need to be willing to take some risks to solve it. For a while at least, we may have to step out of our comfort zones with both each other and the humans."*

Another great silence settled over the animals as each one thought privately about what they'd heard. The first to speak up was Simeon, a gray squirrel who spoke very fast while nervously twitching his big bushy tail the entire time: *"I have an idea."* Then in one breath he added all at once, *"I could take part of my acorns and other nuts I gather in the fall to eat during the cold winter, and yes, well, you see, I could **sort** them!"* Simeon declared nervously as his tail accidentally swatted one of the little Twilly chipmunks sitting too close to him. He finished with, *"And then I'll spread them out on the ground to spell out the human words:*

'O-U-T-S-I-D-E F-U-N F-O-R K-I-D-S!' How'd that be, huh, huh?"

Everyone at once began to clap, flap, squeal, squawk or roar. The noise rose like thunder and then gently softened when a large woodpecker with a bright red head stepped up and said: *"I have an idea too. When I'm tapping my beak as usual on the bark of trees to try and find insects, I'll peck the little holes into human words that say, 'G-O O-U-T-S-I-D-E K-I-D-S."*

A beautiful red-breasted robin piped up next and offered to spell out the same message by spreading around

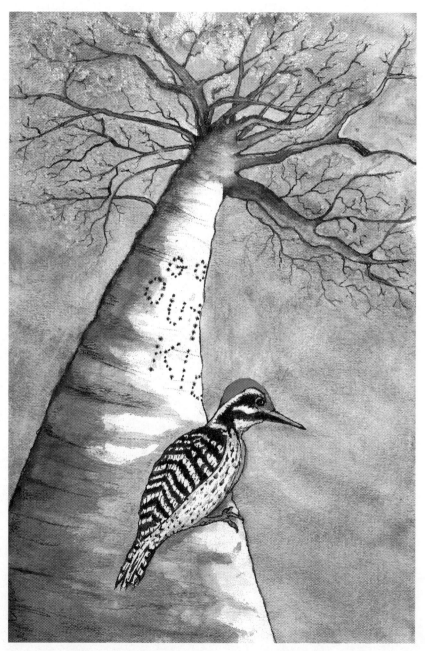

A WOODPECKER'S MESSAGE IDEA FOR THE CHILDREN

the dead earthworms lying on the sidewalks in the early morning after a rain. No one had the heart to tell her it sounded a little gross.

Phineas, a sand crab, who lived on the very beach of their Great Meeting moved into the center of the circle, pinching his claws together a few times to increase the drama before he began: *"I can also do something like the earthworm idea. I live here on the sand with lots of other sand crabs. When the tide goes down and the sand is still damp, my crab friends and I will pinch little holes in the sand to form messages on the beaches! And we can pass the word to many, many others to help do the same!"*

"Yes, and I can send a message too," yelled out a beaver. *"When I'm busy damming up streams by cutting down trees with my teeth, I'll send a message similar to Simeon's and the Robin's. I'll pile little sticks and twigs together to form our message in the sandy dirt at the waters edge."*

A groundhog by the name of Hogo spoke up next: *"I'm pretty gutsy and I often dig my hole and tunnel fairly close to the houses where humans live. I'll leave a flower on the doorstep of as many human houses as I can. I'll increase the number of flowers until I have a path of them leading to good outside places nearby for children to play."* Hogo then quickly added, *"And I cross-my- heart promise not to eat any of the flowers!"*

"I'll help you, Hogo," offered a beautiful, furry rabbit named Slurly-Can-Be, who, by the way, had received her most unusual name because she was so incredibly soft to

A BEAVER SHOWS HOW HE'LL SEND A MESSAGE TO KIDS

the touch. *"And I'll get all the other rabbits to do the same. We'll be the 'Flowers-To-Fun Brigade',"* she said proudly.

Grootor, a canada goose, honked out, *"Everyone knows I fly with my friends and family in a V-formation in the sky (honk, honk). This helps us cut through the wind and fly oh so much easier and faster. But now, at least for a while, we'll fly in a new formation ... a formation of us geese across the sky that spells out G-O O-U-T-S-I-D-E K-I-D-S (honk, honk)!"*

Baylek and Stella were mighty proud of the animals. It was a good start. The Great Meeting resulted in a commitment from the animals to spread the word to as many other animals as they could. It also helped to create an upbeat vibe that felt to the animals like *"We can do this!"*

The animals continued to come up with many clever ways to make contact with humans and move their message forward. For example, many groups of birds began to excitedly plan how they might change their birdcalls to sound more like: *"Every day go out and play!"*

Bunches of parrots came up with their own choruses and pretty soon just about anywhere you went you could hear *"Kids! Play outside in the light, play all day with all your might,"* resounding in the air in the most unexpected of places. Some joined in the animal choruses and thumped their tails or paws in unison to accompany the birds' messages. Eventually, a low drum beat type of sound could be heard with crickets and frogs chirping and croaking in unison, and some birds even fitting their songs to keep time with the drumbeat. It was awesome.

Stella and Baylek also noticed how so many of the animals had grown excited about working as part of a large animal team to turn the nature disconnect trend around and invite children to play outside once again.

Over time, many children and their parents picked up on the messages from the animals. Somehow these humans still possessed a heightened awareness of their surroundings so they got the animals' messages early on and passed them on to others.

And so it went. Faster than a shooting star on a moonless night, the message from the animals spread farther and farther. Pretty soon, the blue-lighted glow Stella had first reported actually began growing dimmer and sightings of children having fun outdoors increased.

Children were spotted lying in the grass looking up at the clouds in the sky playing cloud art with their imaginations. They were heard laughing again as they searched for four-leaf clovers and blew dandelion heads at each other and rolled down grassy hills, their eyes gleaming.

Other sightings included boys and girls having fun outside climbing trees, flying kites in the breeze, chasing big fat bullfrogs, looking under mossy logs, making mudpies, catching fireflies, riding bikes, taking hikes ... much more than could possibly be told here.

For a short time, some people reported they'd seen many animals lined up, sitting on fence posts along roadways or on rooftops and such. They swore the animals looked like they smiled back at them. Then, quick as a wink, the animals disappeared. Back most likely to the wild places they called home.

Many have felt the connection between humans and nature in a spiritual way. Such a wonderfully powerful bond can feed our inner selves. Many of the animals had realized they needed to restore the balance between the world of nature and that of humans. The animals learned this balance must be guarded. It is kept alive and well in part by the joy of children playing outside and growing up with a love of nature inside them, treasuring it as one of life's greatest gifts.

Baylek, Stella and the animals also learned another important lesson. They learned that some things go unnoticed at first, then silently tiptoe into our awareness on velvet bunny paws.

All the animals promised to remain vigilant about the connection between humans and nature. Stella and Baylek volunteered to help watch in the future for any clues that might show children withdrawing once again from the outdoors. They vowed to always keep in touch with the animals about it. What they and the other animals had accomplished together was how legends begin. No one would ever forget it.

So ended the mystery of the blue light when nature spoke through its animals in the wild. Children returned outside for fun and play and made right the world of living things once more.

Juicy Animal Facts From Tale Nine: *The Blue Light Mystery*

Wing feathers—specially designed feathers on the wings of a bird to enable flight; owls have specially shaped wing feathers allowing wind to pass over them without sound.

Food Chain—a series of living things in which each uses the next usually lower member of the series as a food source.

"blue light glow"—the bluish colored glow of light from televisions, computers and other electronic devices.

V-formation—is the particular flight pattern in the sky of a group of birds flying together in a V-shape in which each bird alternates their position to capture the wind to work in their favor and not tire out any one bird more than another.

NOODLE JOGGERS

Tale One: *Ezra*

1. What do you think might happen to Ezra if he were to encounter a flood or was forced to go into a river or lake? Please explain your answer.

2. If you were standing in front, compare your size to a mature chestnut tree back in the 1800's when chestnut trees flourished?

3. Why do you suppose Ezra wasn't afraid of Sally Scott? Do you think most giant tortoises today in the wild are afraid when they come in contact with a human? What about those in enclosures or zoos?

4. In the western states of the U.S., in the fall, do you think elk really might sound like whales?

5. Where might you find giant tortoises today?

Some Possible Answers

1. Because Ezra is a tortoise, he lacks gills for breathing air like fish have; he has lungs like we humans do and he is also very heavy and his movement somewhat restricted by his immense shell; thus, he would drown in water over his head if he could not find something upon which he could float.

2. You would most likely look very small in front of such an enormous tree, somewhat like a hamster might look standing up on his hind legs in front of an adult human.

3. Ezra was likely unafraid of Sally Scott because she showed no aggression towards him. Or, like some animals, he may have sensed her as non-threatening.

4. During the fall in the mountains of states like Pennsylvania, Kentucky, Montana, Idaho, Colorado and Wyoming where there are elk, you can easily hear the male elk, or bulls, calling out to let the females know where they are and to warn other males to stay away. The call is a long, high-pitched whistle-like sound very much like the singing of whales.

5. Most giant tortoises originally came from various islands in southern oceans. Today the only giant tortoises are found in the Seychelles Islands off the coast

of Africa and the Galapagos Islands off of Ecuador in South America. Today in the U.S., there are several types of large tortoises but no giant ones like Ezra and those in prehistoric times. Tortoises have been decreasing in numbers for years. Dramatic decreases began especially during the time of exploration when whalers and buccaneers took tortoises alive on their ships and used them for food like the way we use "canned food" today. Since tortoises are able to go for extremely long periods of time with no food or water, they needed no care on the long, sea-faring voyages of the exploration and colonization era in history. Tortoise meat was a handy food staple on those ocean-going ships and their oil was used for burning oil lamps. Many species of tortoises are threatened with extinction today.

Tale Two: *The Funky Monkey*

1. Do you think the alpha monkey had a choice when he decided to exile Melton? Why, or why not? Please try to explain your answer.

2. Why do you suppose Somat hunted the monkeys at night? Do you think he only ate monkeys? Why or why not?

3. Did you see any life lessons from the story that might help humans to live their lives better?

Some Possible Answers:

1. Yes, the alpha monkey had choices, but the best choice may have been to exile Melton in order to protect the rest of the troop. It also may have been the tougher choice and one for the common good.

2. Many big cat predators are nocturnal or more active at night. Panthers have really good eyesight and would be able to more easily catch a troop of monkeys off guard when they are sleeping at night. Panthers eat all types of mammals and birds because they provide the big cats with more food for the effort it takes to catch them. This means they are *opportunistic* in that they eat whatever animals are handy to catch.

3. When we live together in our neighborhoods, families, and communities it helps us if we have certain rules to keep us safe. There are consequences if we choose, like Smelly Melly, to disregard those rules. Another life lesson is that we often can find courage we had no idea we had.

Tale Three: *The Boy and the Dragon*

1. How would you react if you discovered a giant, legendary animal in distress?

2. Do you think Bo told his parents about Long after he returned home? Why or why not?

3. How would you describe the way Bo first approached the dragon? In what way do you think his approach was effective or not?

Some Possible Answers:

1. There's no wrong answer to this question. All answers are personal and acceptable. What do you think would be your second reaction after discovering the animal? Explain.

2. No wrong answers here either. Maybe Bo just didn't tell his parents right away. Perhaps it would also depend on his relationship with his parents. He might tell them at some point but maybe not immediately if he wanted to continue taking his walks.

3. Bo approached the dragon gently, quietly and slowly, and he also listened to what the dragon was saying rather than rushing in to tell him what to do. This approach was not aggressive and therefore very effective, perhaps a good model to remember when approaching most any animal.

Tale Four: *Charles Bronson and the Crows*

1. Why do you think Charles Bronson, a wild bird, showed no fear of Melinda and her dog?

2. Explain why you think Melinda's rescuing the baby Charles Bronson was the right thing to do or not?

3. Do you think this story was entirely fiction or mostly true? Explain your answer.

Some Possible Answers:

1. Often newborn animals, particularly in birds, will *imprint* or bond with the first animal it comes in contact with, following it around and acting like it's their parent. In this true story, it may explain why Charles Bronson had no fear of Melinda … he had no reason to fear her.

2. It was risky. Rescuing newborn animals is not always successful and often does more harm than good, but in Charles Bronson's case he would have surely died without her rescuing him.

3. This tale is based on a true story and only slightly enhanced.

Tale Five: *The Three Little Caddisflies*

1. Can you think of any other examples of aquatic animals? What is an animal called that lives only on land?

2. Do the caddisflies in the story offer any life principles for us humans?

3. Do you think Trebor was a bully? Might he have also had enemies trying to eat him? Please give an example.

4. The story gives unrealistic human qualities to the animal characters like the larvae thinking and talking. In literature, do you know what that's called? What might be the advantage of using such a technique?

Some Possible Answers:

1. Fish, turtles, clams, tadpoles are *aquatic*; animals who live on land only are called *terrestrial*.

2. Denial, or choosing to disregard reality, can prevent us from doing the work needed to protect us from threats to our well-being. Also, boasting is a foolish waste of time and taunting others is never a good idea, usually not ending well.

3. Trebor's hunting was normal for a predator type of crustacean such as a crayfish, a lobster or a crab. Foxes, raccoons and/or large fish also hunt crayfish.

4. Attributing human qualities to animals is called *anthropomorphism* and can be an effective writing technique to hold the attention of humans, particularly young ones, so they will want to listen long enough to be able to absorb technical information. It often helps to make the story more entertaining.

Tale Six: *Stinky, the Goat Who Would Be Cow*

1. Do you think it's possible for a goat and a young cow to become best friends? Why or why not? Can you think of some examples of other unlikely animals becoming best friends?

2. Do you think the cows in this story had trust issues? Why do you think the adult cows and particularly the lead cow, Clara, seemed to be so serious and hardcore about the "cow rules?"

3. Would it have been possible for Stinky to fix his gas problem? What could he have done?

4. What's another word for the lead animal in some animal groups such as the lead cow, Clara, in the story's group of cows?

Some Possible Answers:

1. Often, when a young animal becomes orphaned, they will bond with another young orphaned animal, whether it is the same kind of animal or a very different one, and they can remain best friends for the rest of their lives. Some examples are a dog and a deer fawn, a giant tortoise and a rhinoceros.

2. Perhaps the cows didn't trust Stinky because he wasn't acting like a cow and it is critically important to their survival to follow the rules and not weaken their defense against predators –their biggest defense is coming together tightly.

3. In reality, no. Stinky may not have been able to fix his gas problem, but he might have learned how it was putting off the cows and walked away when a bomb was outgoing. The lead animal in some groups of animals is generally referred to as the "alpha" and they are highly respected usually because of their age and survival knowledge. In some animals, like elephants and even wolves in some cases, if the alpha is killed the entire pack or herd will be put at great risk if there is no other senior animal to fill the alpha position.

Tale Seven: *The Chameleon's New Smile*

1. In general, what are your favorite top five animals and why?

2. Are you an *omnivore*? If not, what are you with respect to eating preferences?

3. Do you think you could find a fox, a heron, and a chameleon as well as monkeys and raccoons living in the same area today? Why or why not?

4. Where do you think humans are located on the animal food chain? Explain.

5. Can you think of someone who acts like they may have a *"scarcity mentality"*?

6. What do you believe was Niles' new smile?

Some Possible Answers:

1. Answers will vary. All answers are acceptable.

2. Humans can choose to be an omnivore, eating both meats and plants, or we can choose to eat only plants, called being a vegetarian.

3. No. Chameleons whose body color can change may be found near monkeys in the same area today, but they do not exist sharing the same type of habitat area with foxes and/or raccoons who have different needs. One factor to consider is that some animals survive long-term in only particular types of environments with a certain temperature range, etc. While some chameleons can be found in the United States, they do not change colors.

4. For the most part, humans are at the top of the food chain because we have greater intelligence and a powerful advantage from our tools, weapons, and technology.

5. Answers will vary.

6. Niles had always used wit, charm and smiles to win his way, but in the end, his new smile was the body color changes that moved like a smile, only bigger to encompass all of him and keep him safe.

Tale Eight: *White Feathers*

1. Do you think crows, ravens and magpies get together in large groups to have fun, to find food, or for some other purposes? Explain why or why not.

2. Is it believable that a magpie would collect ticks from large scary animals and then hide them in caches (secret places) to eat later? What about mirrors–do you think magpies actually collect mirrors to decorate their nests with like Queenie did?

3. While magpies actually anoint themselves with ants, why do you think they really do this? Why might other animals, like hedgehogs for example, also perform similar strange rituals?

4. Do you think magpie funerals actually happen? Why or why not? Please give examples to support your argument?

Some Possible Answers:

1. Crows, ravens, and magpies are like close cousins, however, they do not socialize, hunt for food or live together for any reason.

2. Magpies do actually collect ticks like the story suggests and then secretly hide them to retrieve later but exactly why is unknown; one can speculate it's just smart to do so. Magpies do seem to have a fascination with mirrors. Many people have observed this phenomenon; however, it is unlikely a magpie nest would be decorated with them.

3. For possible explanations of the magpie self-anointing behavior see the text box of *Juicy Animal Facts From Tale Eight*; however, it most likely has nothing to do with ego and more to do with health and protecting their body from harmful insects, bacteria or fungus. Other animals that self-anoint may do so as part of finding a mate.

4. Magpies actually do conduct funerals like the story describes. It is similar behavior to that of elephants, minus the flowers. While not thoroughly understood, it may indicate these more intelligent animals actually grieve the loss of a family member perhaps because they can recognize the consequences of the loss and feel the emotions from such thinking.

Tale Nine: *The Blue Light Mystery*

1. What were important things the animals knew they needed in order to meet together to try to solve the mystery?

2. Can different animals really have names, talk together and spell out words? If not, why did this story use animals in this way?

3. What leadership traits did Stella and Baylek appear to have that we might learn from?

4. Before the first day of their Great Meeting, what helped to ensure the meeting would be successful when there were so many different opinions and many animals were so worried?

5. What is the most important learning point for you from this story?

6. Might this mystery have been solved another way? Explain.

7. What do you think the "blue light" was that Stella reported? Do you think it had anything to do with the problem of concern to the animals?

8. What do you call it when everyone works together like the animals did to solve a problem? Do you think such an arrangement works better? Why of why not?

9. How did the animals treat each other so that everyone got excited and wanted to help?

10. What do you think may be some of the consequences of kids no longer spending time in the outdoors?

Some Possible Answers:

1. The most important two things the animals needed to solve the mystery were leadership and a plan.

2. No, with the exception of some birds who can be taught tricks to mimic human sounds, animals do not talk like humans or spell as a way to communicate. The story in Tale 9 gives them these fictional, human qualities to help capture the imaginations and attention of its readers and present a real, current social trend at the same time.

3. They were calm. They showed they cared and they listened to everyone. They got the facts and didn't act on assumptions or waste time blaming.

4. They allowed everyone to express their feelings first, and they came up with a peace agreement with each other agreeing to no interruptions or quarreling, etc. so it would be safe for saying what was on your mind.

5. Answers will differ; all are acceptable.

6. Possibly.

7. The blue light referred to the blue glow from electronic devices and televisions. It had to do with the children's greater attention on these devices, passively having fun, instead of actively having fun outdoors.

8. A *team* is when everyone works together like the animals in the story.

9. They were positive, willing to help each other. They thought creatively and did not dwell on the problem but on the solution.

10. Some consequences of kids no longer playing in the outdoors are creating a generation with a decreased appreciation and value for nature and the outdoors. One concern is there will be less support from these children when they become adults to help provide the money and support to organizations who manage and protect our wildlife and parks. If that were to happen, we eventually could lose wildlife and wild places for future generations. Read *Last Child in the Woods: Saving Our Children From Nature-Deficit Disorder,* 2005 by Richard Louv, documenting decreased exposure of children to nature in American society and how it harms children and society. Louv's book examines research and concludes that direct exposure to nature is essential for healthy childhood development and for the physical and emotional health of children and adults.

MORE ABOUT
THE AUTHOR

AUTHOR SALLY SCOTT GUYNN GETS
INSPIRATION FROM GREY WOLF

Sally Scott Guynn, Ph.D., is at heart a consummate storyteller with a passion to influence children to learn about wildlife and nature. Her talent for painting, a lifelong love of animals, her signature sense of humor and boundless creativity complement her impressive experience teaching youngsters in the classroom. Guynn earned a B.A. in biology from the University of Richmond, a masters in science education from the University of Virginia and a doctorate from Colorado State University. All this coupled with a broad, deep career in the wildlife conservation profession created an extraordinary foundation for the author/illustrator to write her first children's book, *The Tortoise Tales.*

Dr. Guynn taught children ages 12-17 in the classroom for over fourteen years. She developed a private elementary school in Virginia, created curricula, and served as the school's administrator for six years. For the next twenty plus years she first shared her expertise with the Virginia Department of Game and Inland Fisheries, heading up and breathing fresh air into that agency's educational programs. Later as a consultant and trainer for both the U.S. Fish and Wildlife Service and the Association of Fish and Wildlife Agencies, Dr. Guynn shared her enthusiasm for wildlife conservation while teaching leadership development, how to deal with conflict, the importance of trust and team building to state fish and wildlife agency professionals across the nation, earning herself a national reputation for excellence.

Before retiring in 2013, Guynn led the creation and establishment of the prestigious National Conservation Leadership Institute, serving as its Executive Director for ten years and receiving notable awards.

The Tortoise Tales is her second book. The author/illustrator resides in her native Virginia and Montana with her husband and her cairn terrier, Maddie B who promises no animals were harmed in the writing of this book.